Scott & Luke Duo

JP Sayle

Editing by Lucas Cornelius
Proofreading by Colette Davison
Book Re-Formatted by Tina Løwén

References to real people, events, organisations, locations, or establishments are only intended to give a sense of authenticity and have been used fictitiously.

Warning

Some of the content of this book is sexually graphic, with the use of explicit language and adult situations involving two males. It is only intended for mature audiences.

Why was finding a Daddy to meet his needs so hard? Could a kink app be the answer to what was missing from Scott's life?

Scott Rainsford is a gentle soul, friendly and hard working. He loves his job as a waiter in the critically acclaimed restaurant La Trattoria Di Amore. On the outside his life looks perfect, but Scott is lonely and craves to meet the one person that will give him what he needs.

Can The App be the answer?

The App offers Scott the freedom to search for the Daddy he has always dreamed of.

It also gives Scott the choice to choose the one man he'd never have expected to want to be his Daddy.

But nothing is simple, a first time Daddy, a broken lift, a phobia and past mistakes make for the perfect stormy start. Can two men, who seem worlds apart, go from enemies to lovers, and meet in the middle?

This is an MM gay romance with Daddy kink, spanking and enough steam to strip paint from wood. With two men that are too complicated for just one book. Warning this book is an HFN.

To all those who love a little extra Kink in their books, I hope you enjoy Scott and Luke.

Thank you to Tina for yet another amazing cover.

Prologue

Scott

Wandering into the staff room, I instantly got the feeling I was interrupting something. Sawyer and Adam giggled and hid Sawyers phone from my view, as if I had superhero vision and could see all the way across the room, but whatever.

"What are you two up to?" I asked, because I couldn't help myself. Adam was my best friend in work and yes, I liked Sawyer, but he tended to keep to himself most of the time. He was also a real hippy, save the planet kind of guy. Once you got him on his soap box you couldn't get him off. As I wasn't, it could get a little tense between us.

"We're just doing some research… for Nathan," Adam said with a mischievous grin crossing his gorgeous face. His hand waved in the air and the overhead lights caught the ring on his finger.

Responding to the grin, I did my best to ignore the ugly twist of jealousy that stabbed at me. I really was happy for him about his recent engagement, and that he'd found his perfect Daddy. Not that we talked about that with anyone. I was the only waiter who knew about what Adam got up to with the head chef and part-owner of the restaurant I worked for. Well, I knew some of it, Adam didn't tell me everything. But I could guess, what with the marks Adam couldn't always hide. Did I mention Carl was a Dom Daddy?

It took a minute to pull my head out of my arse and realise that Adam was talking about the enigmatic Nathan. He was best friends with Carl and owner of a BDSM club called The Playroom. Nathan had been coming for lunch at least once a week for the past month and he'd caused a bit of a stir amongst the single gay men working in the restaurant.

There was something so alluring about the man-mountain, and that's what he was. Tall, blond, with muscles that would put the Rock to shame. He towered over everyone and made me wish I had taken up mountaineering as a hobby.

The thing was he'd never shown any interest in me, not even a flicker. Which was okay, sort of. I'd done a little digging and what Nathan was into was so not my cup of tea. No, I was looking for a Daddy who was into his boy wearing a little lace and silk. Not that I'd had any luck so far, but I lived in hope there was the perfect Daddy out there for me.

On a sigh I tuned back in when Adam poked me in the ribs.

"What ya thinking about? You got a real dreamy look on your face there," Adam questioned, his attention focused solely on me. I couldn't stop squirming when he smirked at the heat now filling my face.

I cursed my pale complexion, it was the bane of my life. No matter what I did to get rid of my milk bottle white skin, nothing worked. Fake tan made me look like a tangerine and can I say, it's so not my colour. The sun only burnt me, then I'd peel and looked like some creepy extra for a horror movie, before I'd be back to where I started.

With my jet black hair and pale grey eyes, I tended to look like a Goth. Not that I have anything against goths, I just want to look a little more like Adam. Bronzed and healthy, rather than like death warmed up.

The nudge to my ribs went from gentle to a full-on dig. "Hey, why are you trying to break one of my ribs?" I asked as I scooted back, rubbing at the now tender spot Adam was still trying to jab at.

"'Cause you're being all vacant and weird. What's up with you today?" Adam asked, his face creased in concern.

Grumbling, I glanced over at Sawyer who was back to looking at his phone, his eyes alight with either excitement or fear, it was a close call as to which.

"There's nothing wrong with me. I'm not the one who's keeping secrets," I nodded towards Sawyer, "and hiding the phone when I walked into the room."

I waited a beat, but when neither man said anything, I walked over to Sawyer. "What are you looking at?" There, I'd asked outright.

His expression became closed off and the phone was shoved into his trouser pocket with such speed, if you'd have blinked you'd have missed it. Now I was really intrigued and desperate to see what all the fuss was about.

I pretended disinterest and went to sit on one of the leather chairs. Seb, our boss, was generous and bought really comfortable leather seats for us to use for our break time. Sitting, I waited to see what the others would do.

Adam gave Sawyer a wink and then headed back out the door, giving me a wave. I glanced at Sawyer, who stood as if undecided as to what he should do.

"Fucksake man, sit and eat your lunch. I'm not gonna annoy you." Even as I said it, I knew that I didn't mean it. They had me intrigued and I really wanted to know what was on Sawyer's phone.

After five minutes of silence, I gave in. "Please." I fluttered my eyelashes, giving my best bashful smile. The one my mother said would get the devil to do what I wanted. "Tell me what you were looking at. I promise I won't say anything."

There was uncertainty, but I could tell he was teetering on the edge. Giving one little push, I said, "I promise not to say anything to the others. You know me, I can keep a secret."

Can I just say, that might have been my biggest mistake, but we'll get to that.

"Alllllright. But I swear if you say anything to anyone I will kick your arse," Sawyer advised, his face pinched into a scowl.

I knew that the threat was genuine. With Sawyer having several different kinds of black belts in all mixed martial arts, you never messed with him. He was really into that shit, and for someone who was all peace and light, it was a big contradiction.

He pulled the phone back out and swiped at the screen, using his thumbprint to open it up. Nice. I was distracted for a moment, wondering if I could do that with mine, when the phone was shoved under my nose.

I'm sure I blinked but I couldn't say for certain. My mind was already way ahead at seeing The App that Sawyer opened. It transported me into a world I was all too familiar with: kink.

My pulse, that had been thrumming away normally, decided it was time to canter. My hands trembled as I reached for the phone.

"Is this a kink app?" I was aware I was being a little dense, but hey. I was trying to get my head around there being a kink app that I didn't know about.

"It is, but it's fairly new. You have to swear you won't say anything." Sawyer clutched at my arm as he spoke. His face pale and his brow pinched so tight he ended up with a monobrow.

With a nod, I offered what I hoped was a sincere smile. "Of course. I would never reveal anyone's secrets, I promise. Cross my heart, hope to die."

The childish saying seemed to loosen the tension in Sawyer's body as he relaxed into me a little.

"What kinks have you heard of?"

The question seemed an odd way to start, but I went with it. "Well, okay. Erm, BDSM of course, which comes in all flavours from vanilla to hardcore. Full submission, to being a slave," I rubbed at my chin. "Then there's Daddy Kink, my favourite, I might add." I offered up that nugget hoping it would show Sawyer I wouldn't judge whatever he was into. "Puppy play, and any other kind of animal play you can think of. There are people who like to act as children, a form of Daddy Kink but just to a different level. I think that's age play. I've heard of people being called Littles, though I'm not one hundred per cent sure on that. I haven't explored that side myself, but I've heard there are couples that enjoy it. Erm… I'm sure there's a load more, but I can't think of any others off the top of my head."

I wasn't sure what part of what I'd mentioned caused Sawyer to wriggle against me and look down at the phone. I got the feeling I might have said something wrong, so I gave his leg a squeeze. "Did I say something to upset you? I didn't mean to."

"No, it's… well…" Sawyer got up and left me with his phone as he stomped around the room, pulling on his multicoloured hair, his dark eyes gleaming.

Before I could say anything he stomped back to me. "I'm what you'd call a little. I like acting like a child and having my partner treat me as such." The breathy confession and small voice got me up off the chair.

Tugging him into my arms, I gave him a hug. The smell of lavender and bergamot wafted up, the familiar scent of Sawyer's homemade body wash.

"Thank you for confiding in me. I promise on my life I won't say a word to anyone about this. What you do in your private life is nothing to do with anyone else." And I meant it. What people did in their private lives was up to them. I don't judge. How could I when I liked my own little added extra kink?

Sawyer pulled back, his eyes searching my face, and what he must have seen allowed his smile to return. "I was a little scared to tell you, well, tell anyone really. I only told Adam because Nathan mentioned to him that I was trialling The App." There was excitement in his voice that wasn't there a few seconds earlier. "It's pretty cool. With Nathan's membership sign-up from his club, and his waiting list, there are more men on here than I thought possible. There are loads of choices, too. Heck I didn't realise there were so many men into what I like." He shrugged. A pink hue covered his face, making him look adorable.

I handed him back the phone I still held on to. "Here, show me. Maybe I could find a date on here. I'd like a Daddy who likes his boy to wear a little lace and silk." Slapping a hand over my mouth, I groaned when Sawyer's eyes sparkled with mirth.

"It's okay. I overshared as well. Let me show you how to search The App. Then we can see if you can find a match."

My heart danced against my ribs at the thought of finding someone. We sat back down as I checked my watch, seeing there was twenty minutes of my break left, I got comfy. "When is Seb expecting you back from your break?"

Sawyer glanced at his phone before looking back at me, "I still have about ten minutes." His lips thinned for a second. "I could download the app to your phone and then quickly show you how to navigate it. That way you can look at it when you have more time. Twenty minutes won't be nearly long enough."

I wanted to do a happy dance across the room, but settled for giving Sawyer a big arse grin, before I went to grab my bag and search for my phone. Seb hated the waiters to keep their phones on them while in the restaurant, not that I blamed him. Who wants to see a waiter messing with his phone in a posh restaurant? No one.

The La Trattoria Di Amore was a small chain of restaurants that were classed amongst the top ten in London. Sebastian Smythe and Carl Bentley had created a reputation for an exceptional dining experience that many struggled to rival. The Michelin stars the restaurant held demonstrated how hard both men worked to make it a popular place to dine.

Any hopes that I might find my dream man while at work had never materialised. No, I ended up with dicks being horrible to me, like Luke Mason. He was the biggest pain in my arse, he seemed to take an instant dislike to me. If I was truthful, when I'd first seen him, he'd totally screamed Daddy to me. Not that I got a chance to find out. One, he has a boyfriend and two, he is a right knob.

Maybe my luck was about to change. I handed my phone over to Sawyer and sat and listened to him explain how the app worked. The fact it was called simply 'The App' was a little odd, but then Sawyer clarified how it was named to prevent people from accidentally finding it. Nathan had The App created for his clientele and his upcoming plans to renovate a part of his loft.

Sawyer got a dreamy expression on his face when he explained that Nathan was going to create a club specifically geared to kinks like his. Distracted about thoughts of how I could sign up for that, Sawyer nudged me twice to bring my attention back to the phone. He started to demonstrate which part of the screen I needed to type in what kink I liked, then it took you straight to where you needed to be.

"That's so cool. Look at all those profiles. Shit there must be over five hundred." I gawked at the never-ending list as Sawyer scrolled and randomly hit on a couple of profiles. There were no face pictures, just body parts, but hey I wasn't complaining.

"See, if you go into the profile it lists their likes and you can press this button here and it will see if it matches yours. Well it will once you add yourself. There is a fee of a hundred pounds to join—"

"Wow, that's a little steep," I said, interrupting his spiel.

"Yes, it is but you'll find it's worth it." With that he carried on, messing with my phone to download the app. Ten minutes later he walked to the door, winking at me as he looked back. "Good luck, let's hope you find your dream guy."

Chapter 1

Scott

Lying on my sofa, I flicked through my phone till I reached The App icon. It was a week since Sawyer had downloaded the app for me, and oh boy he was right. It took me four days to read all the profiles I found for what I'm into. Then it took another two days of whittling them down to the six potential men I was thinking about messaging.

The thing was, I'd never done this kind of dating before and I wasn't even sure how to start off the conversation. With that in mind, I'd called in reinforcements.

The sound of my doorbell dragged me off the couch. The smile lighting my face as I opened the door to Adam, dimmed at the sight of Richie.

Why had Adam invited Richie? This was not part of tonight's deal. My stomach flip-flopped as my hope of making contact with one of the guys on The App by the end of the evening died.

When Adam offered to come round and go through my choices, after I'd moaned at work about how hard it was to make a choice, I thought he'd meant to come alone.

I eyed both men warily. Richie was the boss's boyfriend. Well, in fact both men were the boss's boyfriends' but I was more comfortable with Adam. I didn't really know Richie well enough to say whether we could be good friends. My plans for the evening now seemed in real doubt.

I'd not slept for shit for the last week and tonight was supposed to help with that. I'd been going from excited to utterly terrified at the prospect of trialling a Daddy for a date and having a hook-up.

I stepped back and my face must have shown my disappointment, because Adam gave my arm a pat and started talking. "Stop looking like I stole all Carl's desserts. Richie is here to help as well."

I couldn't really see how that was possible, when Richie had no clue what I was into and had only recently found out he was into men himself. Okay, not men per se, just one man, Seb. Not that I could blame Richie. Seb is a total fox, and deliciously sexy for an older man. He, I might add, also screamed Daddy to me, but I'd never mention that to anyone. It took Seb long enough to be open enough to reveal he liked men.

"Are you just gonna stand there like a dork with the door open all night? I thought you wanted my help on picking a Daddy from the app," Adam said with a big smirk on his face.

Heat coloured my cheeks. I could feel it sweep up my neck so fast there was little I could do to stop it, and with my pale skin I was never going to be able to hide how embarrassed I was. "Thanks man, way to out me. So not cool." I glared at Adam and kept my gaze from going to Richie to gauge his reaction.

"Oh stop, I told you Richie was here to help. He has a Daddy of his own."

I'm pretty sure I pulled a muscle in my neck from swinging my head over so fast to look at Richie, who was blushing and glaring daggers at Adam.

"Thanks for that Adam. You know you can be a right idiot at times?" Richie glanced at me and offered a shrug of his slim shoulders. "There's not much to say after that, but yes, Seb is my Daddy. I'd prefer if you kept that quiet as he's a very private man."

That, I could see, was said purely for Adam's benefit, but he didn't look in the least bit ashamed.

"Okay, I need a drink and then I think you two need to spill." I laughed when Adam held up a cloth bag and the sound of glass tinkled.

"I've already got it covered. I've also told Carl he'll need to come and collect us." He said the last part to Richie, who still looked more than a little pissed.

I rubbed at my neck as the tension in the room increased. "Come on you guys, I need help, not an evening of playing referee," I whined. It seemed to break the stand-off, and Adam slung his arm around Riche's shoulders.

"I'm sorry, but Scott was going to find out sooner or later. All I did was rip off the plaster real quick, so now it's all dealt with."

He gave Richie a big sloppy kiss and got a playful punch to his ribs, but Richie's body relaxed.

"I give in," Richie said, while rubbing at his slick lips. "It stops me stressin', now let's get to the drinking part. I think I'm gonna need it with you two." Richie winked at me and I realised my initial disappointment at seeing him was gone.

"Then follow me, because I really need a drink before we start," I stated, not waiting for the others to follow.

Once we were settled on the seats in the sitting room, with large and way too strong cocktails, and Richie had filled me in on his and

Seb's relationship, I gave Adam the list of guys and their details I'd written down.

Did I mention I'm a little OTT over this? I wrote down each guy's details and what they liked. Then I'd checked out if they'd been on any other dates and if anyone had mentioned them in the chat room that came with The App.

The only one that had no comments was my last choice, DaddyL. There was very little written about him. That was because he was a newbie to the Daddy scene. I wasn't sure what it was about his profile I liked, but it drew me. There wasn't the traditional body part picture like the five others I'd chosen. No, instead he'd used an image of his mouth. His lips were full and a gorgeous dark pink that gave me some crazy hot dreams, though I wouldn't admit to that.

"Hey are you wanting our help, or are you just gonna sit there staring into space?" Adam joked, as his elbow connected with my side.

I jerked, my drink spilling over my hand. "Did you have to do that?" I scowled and got up to grab a cloth to wipe my now sticky hand. I bitched my way to the kitchen and back. "I was thinking about the choices, while I was waiting for you to read their details."

"You do realise we've been sat staring at you for an age, right?"

Richie leant forward and patted my hand as I sat, "Leave him alone Adam, he doesn't need you being a snarky fucker."

"Everybody needs my snark," Adam huffed, though his eyes twinkled with mirth as he took a sip of his drink.

"Soooo, which one do you think I should message?"

"Can I ask you a question?" Richie hesitated until I nodded. "Which one did you read and get the sense they might work for you?"

I chewed on my lip, taking his question seriously. "I was drawn instantly to DaddyL. There was something about his honesty about being new to the scene that appealed, you know? There would be no preconceived ideas. I like that we could be free to explore the potential between us." Something nagged at me as I spoke.

Adam and Richie remained silent, their gazes encouraging me to talk it out. I got up, unable to sit still as I carried on. "I've had two relationships with a Daddy, but neither were very satisfying. I want a Daddy full time, not just in the bedroom, though that would be nice. I get the sense from DaddyL that he might be looking for that too, but I was just reading between the lines."

I took a sip of my drink and stopped pacing to look at both men. "Or he could just be after one scene and a hook-up." The idea soured my mood, but it was a reality I needed to face when trying to find a date through a kink app. There was no guarantee that I was going to get my happy ever after this way, but I was open to anything right now. I'd been single way too long and wanted to find a connection with someone, even if it was only for a few hours.

"Is that what you really want? To have one scene with a Daddy?" Richie asked as he shifted in his seat, an air of concern rolling off him.

"No, not really," I shrugged. "It's been forever since my arse has seen any action and I'd take what I can get. It's not like there are men beating on my door. It feels like I'll never find the right man that fits me." I tried to make it sound like I was joking, but I couldn't conceal the edge of loneliness I'd been trying to keep hidden.

Adam's face dropped right before he stood up, handed his drink to Richie and walked over to me. His hands took hold of my arms, holding me still. "Listen here, you are gorgeous and there is a man out there for you—"

"That's easy for you to say when you have Carl," I turned my gaze to Richie and nodded towards him, "and Richie has Seb." I knew I was being silly but I couldn't seem to stop myself from whining like a baby.

Richie got up and placed the drinks he held on my small wooden Ikea coffee table. He came to me and slung his arm around my shoulders. "We get it. But Adam struggled for well over a year with Carl before he came to terms with their relationship. I didn't do much better. I dicked about trying not to freak out when Adam explained I was out for Seb and that I was maybe a little kinkier than I thought. The point is, it happened in its own good time. We can't force the universe to give us what we want. Things have a way of happening when they're meant to."

I felt really shitty when Richie's face clouded with sadness and I remembered it wasn't that long since his mother had died. "I'm sorry Richie. I should have kept my mouth shut. I'm sorry for what happened to your mum. I don't know how I'd cope if that happened to me."

His arm tightened briefly before he stepped back and picked up his drink, a look of determination on his face. His eyes gleamed in the lamplight. "I got to be there for her when it mattered most and that keeps me going every day. It helps to know she was ready to die in the end. The pain for both of us was too much. I'll let you into a secret, she realised that I liked Seb way before I did and even had a talk with him before she died." He nodded when my eyes widened in disbelief.

I didn't get a chance to say anything, because Adam released my arms and his head spun to Richie. "You never told me that. Why am I only hearing about this now?" His hands went to his hips and his eyes darkened with thunder clouds.

Richie held up his empty hand. "Stop right there, Rambo. Remember you have no room to talk about secrets. Lawyers and Carl, that's all I'm saying."

I could see this was turning into a pissing match, so I interjected. "Hello, I'm right here and you two are supposed to be feeling sorry for my single arse not fighting over who is keeping secrets. Oh and by the way, I'm lovin' all the sharing going on."

Both men froze for a second, before they started to giggle. Seeing the crisis had been averted, I plonked myself down. "Right, back to me, 'cause remember you're both here to help me."

With that, both men sat. Adam grabbed his drink and gave me a toothy grin. "That's right, we are, so let's go through the list of your choices."

My stomach clenched at the devilish glint in his eyes. I could all but see him rubbing his hands together in glee. "I'm not sure I like the way you said that. I'm getting the feeling this was a bad idea."

I glanced at Richie when he chuckled. "You have no idea what you've let yourself in for." With that, Richie picked up the forgotten list and started to read my choices.

Drunkenly, I waved them off several hours later. My mind was trying to comprehend that I'd messaged three of the guys on the list and two had already responded.

Adam concocted the message for me to send, only now, in my slightly inebriated state, I was trying to work through whether drunk messaging was a good idea or not. I staggered into my bedroom as the phone in my pocket buzzed to alert me to a new message. Digging it out of my skinny jeans I squinted at the screen.

Message: DaddyL, *thank you SassyS for reaching out, I'm at work right now, but I'm interested in setting up a meet. I'll message tomorrow.*

It was straight to the point and a silly grin spread across my face. Three for three, woohoo! All the men wanted to meet me. I sank onto the bed and flopped back fully dressed, my eyes drifting closed with the thought of plump lips and what they'd do to me.

Chapter 2

LUKE

Panic gripped my throat the moment I saw the message on my phone. What had I been thinking, signing up for a kink app? I'd no clue what I was doing or why I'd signed up for the stupid thing in the first place.

Really, you don't know?

Ever since my friend Brett mentioned signing up for this new app, I'd been intrigued. With a little research, I'd discovered what Brett was raving about. At a low moment I'd seen no harm in downloading The App and creating a profile. I never thought anyone one would actually contact me, yet here I was with a stupid grin on my face while I was supposed to be being professional at a work function, because I'd received my first message.

"Luke, do you want me to start closing down the bar now?" asked Perry, the head barman.

I tucked my phone back into my pocket, not wanting anyone to see it and figure out what I'd been looking at. The App, though discreet, was still identifiable enough to prying eyes that might then be inclined to go and do a little searching.

"Yes please, Perry," I responded after checking the time. "They haven't requested an extension."

He nodded and walked off to the other end of the bar, where the other staff were waiting.

When the staff started to clear down, I went to find the organiser of the event to say it was time to wrap things up. I searched the ballroom and spotted Mr Rigby tucked in a corner with a hot redhead all over him. Masking my face when I saw it was not the guy's wife, I firmly fixed my smile in place before approaching the couple. It sucked that I actually liked Mr Rigby's wife, they frequently used the hotel for special occasions.

"Sorry to interrupt, Mr Rigby, but it's nearly midnight and, as the ballroom is only booked till twelve, I'm going to have to ask that you wrap up the party. I'll have a word with the DJ for you, if you'd like?"

The drunken nod was followed by glazed eyes that stayed on me for a second, before moving back to the redhead jiggling on his lap. With a sigh, I walked over to the DJ booth and asked that he announce it was the final song.

The school reunion was a success and thankfully there were no significant incidents. Most of the party-goers were staying the night in the hotel, so at least those who'd partaken of the free bar wouldn't have to stagger further than the lifts. My gaze travelled back to Mr Rigby. I shook my head as I watched him give the redhead a room key.

Not your business.

My guts clenched and my hands wanted to ball into fists. I kept them still at my sides. I hate cheaters. Thoughts of my ex filtered past the wall I'd tried to build since his visit.

The unexpected visit made me finally take stock of what was happening in my life, or what wasn't happening.

Isn't that why you downloaded The App?

The reality that I'd been hiding from what I really wanted was an eye-opener no man wished for at the ripe old age of thirty-eight. *Weren't we supposed to have our shit together once we'd got through puberty?*

I was glad when one of the waiters signalled to me, because I didn't need another round of, 'what are you doing with your life?' Or, my best question to date, 'why are you still hiding from what you really want?'

That one kept me on my toes, fuck it made me work harder than a ballerina.

"What is it, Neil?"

Neil explained about some issue with one of the lifts and I ran my hands through my hair.

I loved the hotel that I managed. It was an elite hotel, but with one major drawback: the place was old and with that came all the problems of an old building. The conglomerate that owned the hotel, along with many others, chose this one because of its history and age. The building was beautiful, with many of the original features. Though they'd spent a fortune on maintaining it, it never seemed to be enough. It was, I suppose, the price of having an old building.

However, that didn't help me when things went wrong and needed fixing. Replacing the lifts was high on the agenda for discussion. The old lifts had a habit of breaking down, especially lift three. Fortunately, it was the one least used, tucked down a corridor that many of the patrons didn't use.

I listened to Neil before pulling out my phone to give our maintenance team a call. There was always someone on call twenty-four-seven, because we'd learnt that leaving a guest stuck for hours in a lift did not garner a positive review.

After I'd managed to get the issue resolved and get the stragglers out of the ballroom, so the staff could clear it down and set it up for the wedding the following day, I went to my office. Once there, I shut the door and pulled out my phone to re-read the message.

SassyS: *Hi DaddyL, I've seen your profile and that you're a newbie to the Daddy Kink scene. I'm a sassy boy who loves a Daddy to take charge. Would you be interested in meeting up? SassyS*

My lips spread in a smile and my pulse danced a fast rhythm at what could happen. I sat staring at the screen until it darkened. Should I send another message now, or did that make me look desperate?

Undecided, I swiped at my phone screen, lighting it up as I settled back behind my desk in my leather chair, disregarding how tired I was. I opened the app and searched for SassyS's profile. Laughter bubbled my throat up at the picture of a pair of lacy knickers.

Was that a clue as to what SassyS was into?

I tapped at the screen, pulling up all his information, reading it several times. The buzz of excitement at receiving the message intensified and suddenly I wanted the chance to have a date with SassyS more than I wanted my next breath. After half an hour of staring at the information and when I started to feel a little creeped out by my behaviour, I tucked my phone into my suit trousers as I headed out the door and home.

My mind wouldn't stop, even as I merged with the late-night traffic. With a full day of appointments the next day, I needed to shut off my head.

Parking in my drive, I stared at the empty house and dark windows. I'd yet again forgotten to set the timer for the lights to come on. I hated coming home to a dark house. It always made the loneliness seem that much worse.

Exiting the car, I stopped to inhale the crisp night air. My shoulders drooped as I walked up the path and entered the house. Not bothering to do more than switch the hall light on, I went upstairs and straight to my bedroom. I'd only recently moved from my flat in the heart of London to this house. The two storey, two bedroomed home wasn't big but it was detached, with a closed in back garden, which I'd fallen instantly in love with. I'd needed some space from the hustle and bustle of London, even if it was only a few miles away.

I'd used the time I spent house hunting to stop myself from obsessing and being a real dick over my ex-boyfriend, who I'd been convinced had been cheating on me.

Did I mention I might well have been a real dick? I hadn't taken being dumped on Christmas day, via a phone call, all that well. I'd stupidly flown to where my ex was to confront him, only that didn't go to plan. I'd then come away thinking my ex, Brody, had been cheating with his best friend Aaden. So I did the unthinkable: I hired a private investigator to check out what he was up to. See? I told you, not a nice person.

Unfortunately, it gets worse. I was out walking and came across a dead animal, so I did the inconceivable: I boxed it up and sent it via Brody's PA to him. Yeah, a really shitty thing to do, but in my defence I was going through a personal crisis. My father had recently died and with that came all the past shit I'd buried.

I know it doesn't excuse what I did, and Brody's recent visit brought it all to a head. I sent an apology after Brody came to my office with his boyfriend, who, as it turned out, was not his best friend, but the brother of his friend.

The shock jarred me free from the layers I'd built around myself to protect me from my past and what I'd hidden from for years. I also realised that what Brody had said about it not working between us because he wasn't what I really wanted, was for more accurate than I'd desired it to be. He was right, the only thing hurt was my ego. The split only impacted on my pride and that got me thinking about what I'd been doing and why I was behaving like a complete bastard.

I sat on the edge of my bed and buried my head in my hands. It was a hard pill to swallow when I realised I'd done all this to myself. These last few months, I'd spent time figuring out who I was and working on ways to try and change the things about me that weren't nice.

Shifting to get up, my phone dug into my leg, reminding me that maybe I could have a fresh start. With a sigh, I stood and got undressed, going to the bathroom to shower off the day. Once done, I quickly dried off before heading back to my room and sinking into my bed. The phone sat on the bedside cabinet, where I'd placed it before my shower. Like a siren's song, it called to me to just have one more look at SassyS's profile.

I closed my eyes and ignored the clutch in my stomach. *Go to sleep, the message will still be there in the morning.*

***

The pep talk I'd given myself the night before carried me through a hellish busy day. I got home late again, but at least it was before midnight when I settled in bed with my phone. My plan to message SassyS during the day fell by the wayside, as a packed day and several crises that it would seem no one else could deal with got in the way.

Checking the time on the screen I chewed my lower lip between my teeth. Was it too late to message now?

My fingers twitched with the urge to start typing, so with a shrug, I gave in.

DaddyL: *I'm sorry I haven't messaged earlier, work was hectic so it's prevented me from having time to chat. How was your day?*

I hit send before I could overthink it. Placing my phone down, I tried not to obsess, or recall the message. I'd no sooner let go of the phone when it buzzed.

I won't embarrass myself by saying how fast I picked it back up, or how my hands trembled when I saw SassyS's name.

I swiped at the screen.

SassyS: *It's cool, I'm just home. I had to work a double shift as one of the guys called in sick. Hope you had a good one ;)*

I was aware I probably grinning at my phone like a fool, but as there was no one to see me I didn't care. He'd sent me a winking emoji. I knew it made me a pathetic fool that my heart fluttered in my chest at that silly face, but I couldn't seem to find it in me to care.

DaddyL: *A double shift? That's pretty hard going.*

No sooner had my finger hit send, did I realise what I'd said. Groaning, heat spread up my chest. Fuck, why did I have to type that? I slapped my forehead.

SassyS: *No, there was nothing* ***hard*** *about it.*

I blinked and then my cock started to take notice.

I quickly typed back.

DaddyL: *That's good because Daddy wouldn't like that.*

The slap turned into a full-on thump of my head against the solid wood headboard behind me. The noise rang out as my screen lit up and I am reluctant to admit that I was scared to see what he'd replied. It took several inhales and a stern talking to that he didn't know me, so talking like this didn't matter.

SassyS: *I take that back, I'm hard now.*

Oh shit, oh shit. He liked this flirty play. My cock was totally on board, plump and filled. The head rubbed against the soft cotton of my sheets, as if begging for some attention.

Chapter 3

Scott

My chest was heaving as I waited for DaddyL's next reply. My heart was still racing from reading his last reply and from seeing the picture his response had unlocked. The App appeared to have a nifty extra that allowed users to have hidden pictures, which only unlocked for other users who connected with you. When DaddyL responded to my message, it opened up a hidden picture of his naked chest, with a tie hanging around his neck. That alone was more than enough to have my overtired body stop caring that it had worked a twelve-hour shift. It wanted DaddyL.

The screen on my phone remained blank and I started to panic. Maybe saying I was turned on was not the right thing to say. Second-guessing myself, my fingers began to cramp as I held them still, uncertain if I should say I was joking.

DaddyL: *Is that right? Then be warned, you are not allowed to touch until Daddy says so.*

I groaned so loudly, I was frightened my neighbours below would hear me.

When I'd got home, I'd jumped straight in the shower and was about to put some nightclothes on when my phone buzzed. The minute I'd seen it was DaddyL, I'd lain down naked on top of my duvet and got settled. The pre-cum now leaking from my bare cock and dripping onto my abdomen was making me wish I wasn't alone.

All-day I'd been in a grump, I'd lost count of how many times I'd checked my phone to see if he'd made good on his promise to message me. I'd all but given up hope until the message popped up.

My heart soared way too fast just from a message, and I worried I was maybe jumping in too fast. The other two guys I'd messaged didn't evoke the same need, and I will admit I hadn't bothered to respond to their messages. Was that bad?

Yeah I know, why bother to message if I'm not going to reply? But Adam felt three guys at least gave me choice and the option of going on a few dates to see who fitted best. He'd likened it to buying a pair of shoes, you needed to try them on first before you decided to commit to them.

I heaved a sigh, my cock bucking and reminding me that DaddyL was waiting for a response.

SassyS: *Yes Daddy, I'll be a good boy... but can I touch?*

Aware of the cheekiness of my reply, I waited to see what he'd say. I glanced at the chest of drawers tucked into the corner of my bedroom. The top drawer drew my gaze.

SassyS: *What if it wasn't my hand that made me come, but maybe a piece of silk?*

I sent the message before I could second guess myself. I jumped off the bed and opened the drawer that had been calling to me. I took out a pair of silky underwear and snapped a picture, sending it.

The moment it delivered, the message icon that showed someone was typing lit up. I held my breath. Would he be into boys in girlie underwear?

DaddyL: *Fuck you're asking for a spanking for teasing me. I now understand your profile picture. Though I think I'd prefer a picture of you in those pretty panties.*

I palmed my dick with my empty hand, and squeezed hard to stop the urge to come. Fuck, if he could get me this hot and bothered through chat, what was it going to be like when we met in person?

I got myself under control and sat back down on the bed, not trusting my legs to hold me up. Raw excitement filled me to the point I trembled and struggled to hold my phone still while typing.

SassyS: *Fuck, I nearly came from the thoughts of your hands on me... Daddy.*

I hoped I'd not overstepped with the Daddy comment, but he'd started it. I wasn't disappointed when the quick-fired response came back.

DaddyL: *Remember I will spank you if you come without my permission. Daddy will keep track of your punishments for when we meet.*

That right there got me hyperventilating, I dropped the phone and clutched at my chest, praying that my lungs would start to behave themselves, and soon, before I died and didn't get the chance for DaddyL to fulfil his promise.

My arse twitched and my whole body flooded with warmth. Was I really going to do this?

What if he turned out to be a murderer? That thought pulled me up short. There were daily news bulletins on how people were murdered every day.

I eyed my phone with trepidation, recalling the vetting system The App used. My heart rate, which tripled at the thought DaddyL was a murderer, dropped a fraction at the extensive information that Nathan wanted before you could be added. *That doesn't mean he's not an axe murderer.*

Oh shut up.

I picked up my phone when another message came through.

DaddyL: *I have another long day tomorrow, but I'll message when I get the time. And remember Daddy's words, no touching or coming without my permission. Sleep well sweet boy.*

I stared at the screen for several long seconds, with what I was sure was a dreamy expression on my face. All the thoughts of DaddyL being a murderer were buried under a mushy layer of feelings at being called a 'sweet boy'.

Rolling over, I tugged the duvet from under me and then tucked it around me. The happiness tugged at my lips at thoughts of what was to come.

***

The next few days I lived in constant excitement, always waiting for the next message to arrive. We'd gone from flirty to some pretty intense conversations about what was happening in the world right now. Though he still wouldn't give me his name and hadn't as yet asked for mine, we'd shared a lot about what we wanted from the date we were going to set up. As neither of us talked about what we did for work, it was hard to explain why I couldn't meet him when he was free and vice versa. It seemed the universe was trying to scupper my plans of a hot date with DaddyL.

There was, however, a *lot* of messaging about doing a full-on Daddy scene together. That right there kept me in a state of arousal which was hard to control when I was at work. I'd inadvertently sprung wood when I'd sneaked into the staff room to check my messages and found one from DaddyL, asking me how my day was going.

Yeah, I know it was daft, why would that make me hard? It was the fact he was thinking about me that got me worked up. I turned my back on the staff room door when I heard someone come in.

"Scott, you free to help me set up the small dining room? We have a party of ten coming and there's only one table in there," Adam asked from the doorway.

I turned my upper body, praying Adam wouldn't look down. The tight black trousers I wore for work hid nothing. And a week of not being able to come made it harder to make the bloody thing go down. The mere thought of trying to touch it and readjust made me sweat. "Yeah, give me a sec."

Releasing a loud exhale when Adam only nodded, I watched him head back into the kitchen. I eyed my crotch.

I can do this and not come. I can do this and not come. The voice wittering on in my head lacked real conviction as my hand dropped and tentatively shifted my cock. My thighs automatically clenched at the brief touch. It was too much and not nearly enough. I closed my eyes and worked on picturing the worst thing I could think of.

The recent horror movie Adam talked me into going to see, where there was something that possessed the women living in the house, was finally enough to get me out of the staff room and back into the dining room.

On my way to the small dining room, my eyes landed on one of the men sat on his own with his back to me. My heart thundered in my chest at the sight of the dark, perfectly groomed hair and broad shoulders that filled the pale grey suit jacket. Hands that I knew were manicured picked up the glass of water sat in front of him.

When had he snuck in? I was happy to see Luke Mason was sat in Sawyer's section. The man had taken an instant dislike to me, and for the life of me I couldn't figure out why. I'd never done anything to him, but it was like he was on a mission to make me cry. Though now that I recall, the last two times he'd eaten at the restaurant, he'd been friendlier.

I shrugged off my thoughts when Adam motioned for me from the private dining room doorway. I kept my gaze on Adam and tried to tell myself I wouldn't look at Luke again.

It was a big lie. My head was already twisting to get another glimpse of Luke. There was something so compelling about him, even if he was a horrible shit to me. Again, my Daddy radar screamed that he was clearly Daddy material, though his boyfriend was anything but a boy. Hell, Brody Quilliam screamed dominant and if there was ever a mismatched couple it was those two. But it was none of my business.

"Hey, you gonna stand there all day dreaming or come and help me? The table is booked for one thirty, that only gives me twenty minutes to get the room set up," Adam stated impatiently, his perfect brows pinching in displeasure.

I gave him a smile of apology when I managed to draw my gaze back to him. "What do you need me to do?"

With Adam directing me, we shifted a second table into the room and quickly set up the tables. I stepped back after placing the last gleaming glass down to check everything was perfect. I grinned at Adam, "There, it's perfect."

"It is," he gave me a wink before checking it one last time.

Walking back into the main dining room, I was distracted for a second and ran slap bang into a solid chest. "Oh, I'm so sorry," I said as I stepped back, the scent of Diesel aftershave filling my nose. My gaze moved up the powerful chest and my heart took a nosedive.

"It's fine, I should have been paying more attention," Luke responded, a beautiful smile gracing his gorgeous mouth.

I was sure I looked stupid, my mouth hung open at a total loss for what to say. Having expected to be shouted at, all I got was a pat on the arm and that glorious smile I felt all the way down to my toes, which were currently curling in my shoes. Wow, that smile should be classed as a lethal weapon. He had nothing on Mel Gibson in that film. He may be able to drop you with a shot, but that smile would do the same.

When I found myself staring after him, not at all convinced I wasn't drooling, I wiped at my chin. Pleased to find it dry, I went off to the kitchen in a daze. A thought niggled that I was missing something, but I couldn't think what.

What the hell was wrong with Luke? Maybe he'd been kidnapped by aliens and they'd messed with his head before sending him back. It had to be that, because in the three years he'd been eating at the restaurant, not once had he smiled at me.

Obsessing about it, I went in search of Sawyer. I found him in the kitchen waiting on Billy, Carl's second in command. I walked over to him and tugged him away from the counter. Checking no one was in earshot, I asked, "Do you think Luke Mason is acting weird today?"

His eyes widened, "You noticed too? He was so bloody smiley today I had to keep checking he wasn't having some sort of breakdown. You know when you see those people that get a manic smile that isn't really real, right before they have a breakdown? I saw this woman once on the news, she looked like that. It was freaking me out man." Sawyer shuddered.

"Yeah. I know what you mean. I just bumped into him—"

"And you lived to tell the tale?" Sawyer asked, jumping in before I'd finished, his eyes flashing with alarm as they travelled over me.

"I'm stood here aren't I,"—I rolled my eyes—"so I must have survived. I did wonder if maybe aliens abducted him and messed with his head. Oh, or better yet, replaced his personality with a new improved one."

I smirked, then hunched at Seb enquiring, "You wouldn't be talking about one of our clients would you?" His dark brows lifted and his face went all stern.

I mumbled an apology as Sawyer said, "There is something fishy going on with Luke Mason. He's all nice and friendly. When has he ever been like that, I ask you?" His hands came up and waved in the air.

"You may be right, but gossiping about our clients is not okay. And I'd suggest you steer well clear of him." The subtext was explicit, stop now. But the underlying warning confused me. Seb looked genuinely concerned about Luke.

Before I could think about it further, Billy advised the meals were ready so I took a couple of the plates and followed Sawyer out of the kitchen into the serene dining room.

I leant into him the minute the door closed behind us. "What was that all about? Did you catch Seb's concern?"

He nodded and whispered back, "You couldn't miss it. But I have no clue what it's about." With that, he walked off to deliver the food and I followed, replacing my frown with a smile for the clients.

I didn't need to be worrying about Luke. It had nothing to do with me.

Chapter 4

Luke

I kept my hands from clenching, even when the tingling from touching Scott remained after the brief contact. What the hell was wrong with me? My body's reaction to Scott was so fast I'd had no time to process. My arms were full of the pretty young waiter before I could think about what I was doing.

I'd seen he was going to knock into me and instead of moving out of the way, I'd let him fall into me. The harebrained idea was rebounding now that I was stood at the curb, waiting for a taxi with a raging hard-on that wouldn't quit. *What was wrong with me?*

I recalled the first time I'd walked into the restaurant with a friend who'd suggested we dine in there. He'd been raving for weeks about the place, saying the Italian food could not be beaten, that it was like having a small slice of Italy in London. I'd thought he'd been exaggerating until I ate the pasta special of the day. I could still remember the creamy sauce setting my taste buds alight.

It wasn't the only thing that set your taste buds alight though, was it?

I sagged under the weight of my thoughts pointing out the obvious. The moment I'd laid eyes on the dark-haired, pale-skinned, trim waiter, I'd felt an itch that for years I buried under the baggage my father put squarely on my shoulders.

It sat there weighing me down, and I found myself snapping at the young waiter. The tears shining in his eyes were ruthlessly ignored. It set a pattern that resulted in Seb twice speaking to me about my behaviour. They were not my proudest moments. The shock on Scott's face when I'd smiled would have been funny if it were not for the reason it was there. I was a shit, and though the last two times I'd been in to eat, I'd made a real effort to be kinder, to show I wanted to make amends, it would seem I'd need to try harder.

The honk of a horn jerked me from my thoughts and I slipped into the back of the taxi, not dwelling on the stale, sweaty odour coming from the front of the cab.

I gave the address of the hotel and sat back, watching the slow-moving traffic through the window. The dismal grey sky matched my mood. *How do you change people's opinions?*

Who knows?

I wanted to sigh, but I refused when this was all of my own making. I glared at my still semi-erect cock. I was confused as to why Scott got me worked up, when I'd been more than happy to set up a date with SassyS.

Maybe it was because of all the time I'd spent fantasizing about SassyS, that I got hard from touching Scott. He screamed boy to my inner Daddy. I chewed my lower lip between my teeth. *Was that really why?*

I was working on being more honest with myself and I knew damn well I'd always been attracted to Scott. *So what do I do now?*

As if Scott would want to go on a date with you? You saw his face, you'd be the last person he'd want.

This time I did groan. Would going on a date with SassyS be a shitty thing to do, when I fancied someone else as well? I definitely wanted SassyS, and that was without seeing him. He was funny, bright, and often a ray of sunshine in my day when he messaged, even if it was only to say hello.

Where does this leave me?

Set up a date and see what happens, that's where it leaves you.

Not able to argue with myself any longer, I pulled out my phone and opened the app.

DaddyL: *You mentioned that you have a day off next week on Thursday, do you fancy meeting me?*

Hitting send before I could change my mind, I was a little disappointed not to receive a response by the time the taxi pulled up outside the hotel. Paying the driver, I stopped at the door to chat with Rupert, the doorman. We talked about his family; his wife had been suffering from a recent cold, which had turned into pneumonia.

He'd been with the hotel for more than forty years and often said he'd learnt more about life and people by just watching the world go by. I often wondered what he thought about me. He was always friendly, but slightly reserved.

After a couple of minutes, I bid him goodbye and went off to deal with whatever was waiting for me in my office. The afternoon flew by and before I knew it I was home, sat in front of the telly, brooding over why SassyS still hadn't responded.

Didn't he want to meet face to face?

We'd talked about it, but as yet our work schedules hadn't permitted it. And though next Thursday I'd still need to work, I had gone through my diary and moved several meetings so I could be free if SassyS agreed to meet. Hell, I'd even booked one of the most expensive suites in the hotel so I could spend a little time getting to know him in person.

As if that's the only thing you want to do to him.

I sighed. All the flirting back and forth and the way I slipped into being a Daddy allayed my fear I wouldn't be comfortable being that way in front of someone. *Yeah, but you haven't tried it yet.*

I got up and threw the phone I'd been clutching in my sweaty hand onto the sofa and went to get a drink. The desperation and antsy feeling in the pit of my stomach left me undecided as to whether having an alcoholic beverage would be a good thing. I could taste bile at the back of my throat. Going to the kitchen cupboard, I took out a glass and filled it with some water instead.

The water splashed all over the counter as I darted for the door faster than a sprinter off the blocks. The sound of my phone buzzing was like the starting gun that let me loose. With wet fingers, I grabbed for my phone as I landed on the sofa in a heap, my chest heaving.

Bloody hell, pull yourself together man. My head shook at how I must look, panting and sweating over a message. I was pretty positive if anyone saw me right then, I'd be looking rather desperate.

With trembling hands I swiped at the screen and all my worries fled at seeing SassyS's name on it. I fumbled to unlock the phone while attempting to calm my breathing.

SassyS: *I'd love to meet. Just tell me when and where and I'll be there.*

The underlying enthusiasm quelled the worry eating at my control. I quickly typed back.

DaddyL: *I work in a hotel, maybe you'd like to meet there and we can use one of the hotel rooms?*

I hit send before I could chicken out. Was I being too presumptuous?

The screen lit with another message.

SassyS: *That would work, but how would we do this? Will you want your work colleagues to know you're meeting me for a...*

The smile I'd been struggling to contain, fell from my lips. What were the dots about? And what had it got to do with my work colleagues?

I frowned down at the phone, when it suddenly dawned he didn't know I managed the hotel.

DaddyL: *I manage the hotel, so it doesn't matter what anyone thinks.*

There I'd laid it out.

SassyS: *Wow, you manage a hotel? Fuck, I'm feeling a little inadequate here.*

DaddyL: *Stop that right now. It's a job, nothing more. It pays the bills.*

SassyS: *Okayyyyy... I can all but hear you growling at me.*

Grinning, I typed out another message.

DaddyL: *Damn straight you can, that might just garner you another punishment. What number are we up to now? Four.*

SassyS: *It's a good job you can't see my face Daddy.*

He'd used the rolling eye emoji on more than one occasion, so taking a guess, I messaged back.

DaddyL: *You're rolling your eyes and that's punishment five.*

I waited to see what he'd do.

SassyS: *Daddyyyyyy you're making me hard and I'm at work. And you're right I was rolling my eyes... I still am ;)*

I roared with laughter at his cheekiness. Fuck I couldn't wait to spank his arse. My cock was more than happy with the imagery floating through my head when another message came through.

SassyS: *Gotta go back to work... pray for SassyS's survival. At this rate, my balls might drop off with how blue they are.*

With that the messages stopped and I sat grinning at the TV like the idiot I was.

The one that needed praying for was me, because the warmth flooding my chest spoke louder than any typed message. I was falling for the sassy boy. I just hoped that when we met he wouldn't be disappointed in me.

The smile left my face. I glanced up at the ceiling. "If there's a God up there, please let him like me. I swear I'm working on showing the real me." My head rested on the back of the soft sofa pillow and I shut my eyes, trying not to think too hard about the tears welling in my eyes.

Chapter 5

Scott

I raced to hail a taxi, my arm flailing in the air as my nerves took hold. Was I really doing this? It would seem I was, as a cab stopped and I jumped in, giving the driver the address of the hotel I was meeting my hook-up at.

Ever since Sawyer uploaded The App to my phone three weeks earlier, I'd wondered if I'd go through with actually meeting someone. The fact I'd spent all my free time messaging DaddyL, said I was more than keen.

Daddy kink was something I'd stumbled upon when a childhood friend and I were searching the net for porn. Yes we were a mere fourteen, but what can I say? Boys will be boys. What we found left me hard and interested in learning more about Daddies.

Don't get me wrong, I had no craving for a father figure, I have a great bond with my parents. There are no skeletons in my wardrobe, none. I just liked the dynamics of that kind of relationship. The idea of being cared for and having someone make all the decisions, with maybe a little punishment for being naughty, made me yearn in ways I never had before. I came to accept that this desire was just a part of who I am.

The problem was, I'd not found that person that fitted my ideal. My past two real relationships with a Daddy, though an enjoyable dynamic, had been a little flat. They'd been reluctant to take it to the level I needed. I wanted them to treat me as their boy all the time, not just in the bedroom.

There was also my need to sometimes wear feminine underwear. It was an essential part of who I am. I loved the feel of the satin and lace against my skin. I'm an odd mix of contradictions and I felt like this might be why I've been single for over four years, since my last Daddy found my needs too much.

With a groan, I shut my eyes, not needing to add to my nerves with thoughts of my past relationships.

It's only a hook-up, not a lifelong commitment. If I kept saying it, it might sink past the need for it to be more. *Yeah, right.*

I rolled my eyes at my own needy thoughts.

We'd finally managed to agree a date, though we still hadn't exchanged names. And though I'd divulged my initial and surname so I could collect the room key for the hotel room he'd booked, DaddyL explained he wouldn't reveal his name until we met in person.

Excitement coursed through my body at the reality of that happening today. The flirty messaging since I'd tapped his profile kept me on tenterhooks. He said he was new to Daddy kink, and though initially I'd been a little sceptical about meeting a newbie, he'd slipped right into the role more quickly than I'd anticipated. I'd worked on the proviso that if it didn't work, then I didn't have to see him again. Though, that thought often made my stomach twist into terrible knots.

The taxi stopped outside one of the poshest hotels I'd ever seen. *Oh fuck, this can't be right.* "Is this the Worthington Hotel?"

"Yeah mate, that will be twenty seven pound forty," the guy said, not looking my way as he spoke.

The anxiety that had been riding my arse pretty hard since I'd made the date decided to gallop to the forefront. My hands trembled as I tried to fish out the money from my pocket. Chest heaving, I blinked and prayed I wasn't about to have a panic attack in the back of the taxi.

Sucking in a deep breath, I managed to find the cash and hand it over. Actually getting out of the taxi? Yeah that would be a little harder with my knees knocking together.

I'm not sure how long I sat looking out at the austere hotel before the driver poked his head through the small glass window. "Hey, you alright back there?"

Wanting to say no, I nodded instead and with clammy hands I opened the door and stepped out of the taxi, after thanking the driver. He didn't give me a chance to do more than step away before he took off. Shoving my hands into my jeans' pockets, I eyed the dude stood outside the massive glass doors.

The posh outfit and top hat gave me a sense I should have made more of an effort with my clothing choices. I'd paid more attention to the lacy underwear I was wearing than to the jeans and black fitted top I'd pulled on over my underclothes.

The urge to run away and forget the whole thing weighed on me. Could I go through with this? Two weeks I'd been building myself up to this moment and now I was here, I wasn't sure I could walk through the hotel door. The fact the place was so posh wasn't helping my cause. Shit, he managed this place. He was so out of my league!

How was I going to manage to go to reception to pick up the room key he'd left for me? I kicked at the ground with my scuffed trainer and scowled at how I thought meeting in a hotel was a good idea. When he'd suggested a hotel, it appealed because that meant we were both free to go without the awkward moment of someone having to ask the person to leave. Or, God forbid, you overstay your welcome.

Now however, in the light of day, I wasn't so sure this was the best idea. This guy managed a posh hotel, and I was a mere waiter. My mother often called me a heathen, posh is so not my thing. I might work in a well to do restaurant but that was different.

"Sir, are you all right? Can I help you with something?" The tall dude stood by the door, unnoticed by me, had walked towards me. His face was a neutral mask, though he sounded a little concerned. I wasn't sure if he thought I was up to something, or if he was picking up on my panic.

I gave the best smile I could summon. "Erm…well… you see… I'm meeting a friend here." I stopped, realising if the dude asked me for the friends name I really couldn't say DaddyL.

"Have you been here before, Sir?"

I shook my head. I mean really, do I look like I frequent this type of hotel?

"The reception is on your left as you go through the door. I'm sure one of the staff will direct you to where you need to meet your friend." As he spoke he stepped back to the door, opening it and encouraging me into the foyer.

My feet moved reluctantly and as the door shut at my back I heaved out a loud sigh at the gorgeous surroundings.

Why did I think this was a good idea again?

The place was beautiful, all gleaming glass and wood. The building was old, but was beautifully maintained with a lot of what had to be the original features. Massive chandeliers hung from the ornate cornices on the ceiling. There were stunning murals painted on the walls and ceiling. The seats scattered about were plush navy velvet and matched the carpet. The air was scented with expensive perfumes.

My mouth dried at the people walking around or sat in chairs. I stood out like a sore thumb, my scruffy outfit screaming imposter.

With a sweeping glance of the foyer, I spotted the reception desk. Could I do this? I glanced over my shoulder and saw the guy outside staring at me. His face was creased with speculation and something that made my feet take me to the reception. There was no way I wanted the guy following me inside to see who I was meeting.

At the desk, I stood and waited for one of the three receptionists to become free. I heard the chatter, but didn't really pay any attention to what was being said, I was still too busy having a personal freak out.

"Good afternoon, sir, can I help you?" a sing-song voice asked, and when I glanced at the blonde with a pretty smile, I forced my head to move.

You can do this.

Stepping closer to the elaborate wooden desk, I offered what I hoped was a confident smile. "I'm collecting an envelope. The name on it is S Byers." I'd given my initial and surname so I could collect the room key after much discussion about how we were going to do this. So I was confident I was at least not making a fool of myself. Well, that was if he hadn't changed his mind and there was no key for me.

Unaware of my personal meltdown, the woman replied. "Please hold on sir, while I go and see if I can find it for you." She bustled off to a counter at the back to search through some drawers.

Sweat coated my top lip. Before I could swipe at my face, she was back with a white envelope in her hand.

"Here you go, sir. Do you need anything else?"

"No thank you, that should do it." I took the envelope and instantly realised it wasn't a key card but a key inside. Wow! They still used old fashioned keys for the rooms.

I walked off, then remembered I'd never been in the hotel before, so was not sure where the lifts would be. I glanced around, but not seeing anything obvious, I wandered around. Seeing nothing obvious, I walked towards a broad set of doors, and poked my head around them.

There was a long empty corridor and a sign with 'lift' written on it. Relieved that I didn't need to go back to ask anyone, I walked through the door and down the corridor until I got to the lift.

My heart skipped a beat at the thought of getting in the small box. For years I'd suffered from claustrophobia after friends thought it would be funny to shove me into a wardrobe and lower it to the floor and trap me inside. Those five minutes of being trapped inside that box gave me years of nightmares. I've never been able to cope with being shut-in, at least not for any significant amount of time.

Reassuring myself this was only going to be for a minute, I pressed the button to summon the lift with a trembling finger. There was no way I was going to walk up to the sixteenth floor and turn into a sweaty mess, so this was my only option.

You can do this. You can do this. I chanted as the doors opened and I stepped into the box.

"Hold the lift, please," a voice called from the hallway.

I gripped the brass bar encircling the lift walls as I felt the colour drain from my face. *No fucking way!*

Chapter 6

LUKE

Running down the hallway, my hand raked through my hair trying to tidy it. I clutched the bag I'd retrieved from my office, for my afternoon of fun.

Though with the way my day was turning out, my date probably wouldn't show up. It had been one disaster after another the whole morning, and all I could do was pray that that was it for the day. I'd wanted to be up in the room, ready for when my date arrived, but as I checked my watch I could see I was already running a few minutes over the time we'd planned on meeting.

I pushed through the doors leading to the lift and caught the back of someone walking into it. I raised my voice so the person who'd stepped into the lift could hear me. "Hold the lift, please." I didn't want to have to spend ten minutes waiting for it to return.

The lifts were one of the many things that were always on my agenda for an upgrade. And the one that was now waiting for me tended to misbehave the most.

I went to smile as I stepped into the lift to thank the person for holding the door, but it froze on my face. Blinking, my mouth opened then shut twice before I could speak. "What are you doing here?" It came out as a husky demand, and I cursed for not keeping better control of myself.

The gorgeous waiter from my favourite restaurant stood stock still, staring at me with undisguised anger. Not that I could blame him. Even after our last encounter when I'd tried to be friendly, I seemed to miss the mark by a mile.

"It's none of your business why I'm here. I'm not at work now, so I don't have to be nice to you." His voice trembled and the sulky tone were more than enough to stir up the arousal I usually felt when I was anywhere near him.

I stepped into the lift to allow the door to close. The space seemed to shrink as the scent of Scott's cologne took up all the air. Inhaling was the worst idea, my cock twitching as my senses swam in the delicious smell.

Fuck a duck, this will not do. I eased back and leant against the mirrored wall. *You're meeting a guy for a date, so let it go,* I reminded myself, even as my trousers tightened further over my groin.

"What floor?"

My mouth dried up, preventing me from saying any more. Waves of lust were attacking me, derailing any thoughts I had of meeting SassyS. Sorting a date through The App now seemed like the worst idea, with the man I'd dreamed about on more than one occasion stood not more than two feet from me. I'd thought with the attraction building between me and SassyS, I would have been able to let go of my attraction to Scott. It seemed not!

"The sixteen floor, please."

The please sounded more like a fuck you, but my gut was too busy tying itself in knots to think about that. The sixteen floor was where I was going to meet SassyS. I got an itch at the back of my neck and my intuition screamed this was no coincidence. SassyS, was the S for Scott?

I found myself asking, "Are you booked into the hotel? I wasn't aware you liked to stay here?"

Scott's already pale face turned a horrible shade of grey while his hands shoved into his pocket. I caught sight of the envelope in his hand before it disappeared from view.

My heart sank. No, it can't be Scott who I'd made plans to meet, surely the universe wouldn't do that to me?

Needing to know if I was right, I stepped closer to Scott and tried not to breathe too deeply. "What room are you staying in?" I locked my eyes with his silver gaze and used my most dominant tone. His lashes fluttered as his pupils dilated.

His pink tongue flicked across his plump lips making them glisten wetly under the lights. "I'm... in..." His face filled with confusion as he dug out the envelope. His gaze moved to his hand before he defiantly looked back at me. "1681, not that it's any of your business," he said belligerently as his chin poked out, challenging me.

Oh that would not do.

My hand clenched the bag I held, as the reality of who I'd made a date with sank in. All the flirty chat I'd engaged in, along with all that I'd revealed about my needs, came back to slap me in the face. Would Scott run when he learned I was his date?

Tempted to blurt it out and ask, I clamped my mouth shut. *Think damn it.* Should I just let him go to the room and delete my profile and pretend I'd never heard of The App? Or should I face what I'd known about myself since my father started to demand I act like the man he wanted me to be?

What, a man that many people disliked? Yeah go back to that because that really worked for you.

And wasn't that the problem? My father's influence was so ingrained on what I presented to the world, I'd forgotten who I really was underneath the veneer.

I'd never hidden that I was gay. From the moment I realised I was into guys, I'd told my parents. They'd always been supportive of everything I'd done, so I didn't expect me being gay to change that. How wrong I'd been! My father turned into a macho arsehole. His idea of what I should be was something that was drilled into me, somewhat painfully at times.

So the side of me that wanted to embrace being a Daddy was hidden under the macho bullshit my father expected from me. It dictated how I'd dated, going for men built similar to me so as not to appear weak, when those men were the exact opposite of what I'd wanted.

The only problem was, even after the death of my father, it was too ingrained to switch off. I'd made some stupid arse decisions because of it, and after Brody's wake up call, I was still trying to figure out who I really was without all the pressure to be something I wasn't.

This was supposed to be my first step.

The tension was so tight across my shoulders, I thought my trapezes muscles were going to snap at any moment. As I kept my gaze on Scott, my thoughts raced through my mind. *What should I do?*

My mind wanted an answer to the question. My cock, on the other hand, was impatient and chose an answer for me. I stepped into Scott's space, towering over him. I took hold of the chin still pointing at me with firm fingers. "A Daddy would spank your bottom for acting like a brat. Is that what you're after, Scott?"

He jerked. His whole body shuddered, his eyelids lowering to half-mast. Then he sucked his lower lip between his small white teeth.

With no chance to demand an answer, I was jerked off my feet by the sudden halting of the lift as it juddered and made an awful screeching sound. I knocked into Scott, pushing him into the mirrored wall behind him. His wail was lost under another loud clunking noise before we came to a grinding halt.

"Bloody hell! Can this day get any worse?" I scowled and complained to Scott as I shifted off him and righted us both. It was only then that I noticed how his eyes had glazed over and that the pulse at his neck was bouncing so fast it made him look like there was something wrong with his neck.

"You okay? The lift does this occasionally. It's nothing to worry about." I patted at his arm, only he wasn't paying me any attention. His eyes were firmly locked on the lift door. Sweat gathered on his upper lip as he remained totally still.

A ball of panic gathered in my throat, and I swallowed. The fear on Scott's face turned my stomach to lead. Oh shit, he was scared. Was it because of the way I'd behaved?

Uncertain how to broach the subject, I turned my attention to calling for help. I opened the small door that housed the telephone to call for assistance. When Bob the maintenance man answered, I let out a relieved breath. "Bob, lift three is bloody stuck again between floors,"—I glanced at the panel—"nine and ten."

I listened to him waffle on about what he thought might be the problem, until I heard a sob come from the side of me. My gaze shifted from the panel to Scott. His face was stark with terror, his body shaking with uncontrollable sobs.

Fuck! Fuck!

I shut Bob up mid-sentence, "Bob, just assess what needs fixing and ring me back to advise how long I'm going to be trapped." I was already putting the phone back before he answered.

With the phone down, I realised my mistake in using the word 'trapped' as Scott's legs gave way and he fell in a heap to the floor.

The heart trying to escape my chest made my hands tremble and I dropped the bag I'd forgotten I was still holding. I reached for Scott, unsure what I should do, so I went with my first instinct. Sitting down next to him, I pulled him into my lap and held him close.

Gently rocking him, I soothed him. "Come on, sweet boy, it's going to be alright. Shush now, you need to stop crying and listen to… me." I stopped myself from using the word Daddy, though it sat on the tip of my tongue. As I wasn't sure if it was my behaviour or the lift stopping that caused Scott to become a blubbering mess, I needed to tread carefully. I didn't want to make things worse.

As if it could get any worse?

No sooner had the thought popped into my head than the phone rang. As I shifted to grab it, Scott clutched at me. His teary eyes lifted and begged me not to leave him. Something inside my chest opened and warmth flooded through me. *Ah shit.*

Why did I have to have feelings for him? Why?

"I'm not letting you go sweet boy, I just need to answer the phone." With a watery sigh he released my shirt so I could stretch up and grab the phone.

"Yes, Bob?"

"Bossman, it's not good news. The part I think I need to fix the drive shaft, I don't have. I've rung our suppliers and they have one, but it's a four-hour drive away. I've asked them to get a courier to bring it. But my best guess is you're gonna be stuck in there at least six hours, maybe more if the delivery guy gets stuck in traffic." Bob's need to always go with the worst-case scenario, received a gasp and a loud sniffle from Scott who must have been able to hear the conversation.

Not responding to Bob, I whispered in Scott's ear without thinking, "Don't worry, Daddy is here. I'll take care of you and keep you safe."

Chapter 7

Scott

The rollercoaster I was riding needed to fucking stop, right fucking now. I'd thought that there was nothing worse than Luke Mason stepping into the lift. I'd been wrong. First, the way he was acting was making my head spin as it tried to catch up with this new phenomenon. Then, when he'd uttered the word Daddy, my cock tried to fight its way out of my lacy underwear to show him how much it wanted a Daddy. And that was if you didn't take into account that the lift broke.

The well of panic that I was drowning in felt so deep until I found myself held so gently and rocked against a solid wall of muscle that smelt like heaven.

Then I heard Luke say, "Don't worry, Daddy is here. I'll take care of you and keep you safe," and my heart melted faster than ice in a drink on a hot summer's day. It smothered the overwhelming panic as I struggled to cope with all the emotions racing through me. So I did what I always do when I'm overwhelmed, I hid.

Sticking my wet face against Luke's neck, I inhaled his aftershave and let the scent block out everything. My senses swam from the masculinity of it. Nuzzling into the warm flesh, wanting to immerse myself, my body relaxed. The moment I let go the arms around me tightened and I was rewarded with a gentle kiss to the top of my head.

A flush rose up my face at how treasured I felt.

"Scott, look at me." Though the command was spoken softly, there was an element of authority that was undeniable and I wanted to obey.

Sucking in one last deep breath, I raised my head. Blinking the tears from my eyes, Luke's beautiful face filled my vision and left me breathless. "Yes..." I quivered with an urge to say more. But I wasn't sure I could, not when Luke and I had so much history.

He might be being kind to me now, but I'd been on the receiving end far too many times of his cutting words at work. The number of times he'd reduced me to tears were countless. I knew I shouldn't let him get to me and it took several months to figure out. It upset me because underneath it, I really wanted him to like me.

Daft, I know, but there was something so compelling about him, I was drawn to him like a moth to a flame. Only I really didn't want to get burnt.

I had a feeling that was about to change. My mind had worked out the second Luke asked what room I was booked into, that I'd somehow ended up with a date with the one person I'd least expected: Luke Mason, my nemesis from work.

"Have you figured out who you're meeting today?" The simple inquiry held such weight, I wasn't sure how to respond. His eyes demanded I be honest, and also threatened something if I wasn't. The threat dried my mouth and I nodded for fear of not being able to get the words past my thick tongue.

"Good boy. Thank you for being truthful with me. The question is, do you still want to go ahead with this… date?"

Unsure why he'd hesitated, I chewed my lip between my teeth. Did I want to have this… date?

Now that I knew it was with Luke, shouldn't that make the answer easy: no? The very idea of uttering the word no gave me palpitations.

Thoughts and worries flew out of my head as the floor beneath us jerked. My arms clung to Luke as my eyes flew to the closed door and reality came crashing down on me. "I have to get out. You need to get the door open now. I can't stay in here. I can't, the walls they're closing in on me. Oh God help me," I gasped with a strangled moan. My fingers curled tightly into Luke's jacket, clinging on for dear life when the lift shifted again and my vision wavered with black spots.

"Scott, stop that. You are safe, look at Daddy, and breathe for me."

Head lifting at the sharpness of Luke's voice and the term Daddy, I sniffed up and tried to stifle the sobs in my chest, while sucking in several breaths. "I'm not sure I can... Daddy," I warbled and did my best to try and do as he asked. But the fear gripping me wasn't deterred by the demand.

My fear was on a mission to escape the reality we were trapped for what potentially could be for hours in this box. A box that right now, didn't feel all that safe with the jerking movements it kept making.

"You're not listening to Daddy. I want you to keep your eyes on mine, boy."

When firm fingers took hold of my chin and lifted it, I realised I'd moved my gaze back to the lift door. "I'll have to punish you if you disobey Daddy again. I asked you earlier, is that what you want, for Daddy to spank your bottom?"

A shiver rolled down my spine, only this time it was nothing to do with fear. Hell no, this was everything to do with the idea of Luke touching any part of me with his hands, of him seeing what I wore under my clothes.

My lips trembled with the urge to say "yes," but I kept silent, waiting to see what he would do next.

"I need you to answer me, sweet boy." His nostrils flared as his dark eyes narrowed on mine.

"I don't know... Daddy." It was the truth, I was undecided. My body was totally on board with where this might lead, but my head was struggling to switch from this Luke to the Luke that took pleasure from humiliating me in front of other people. Could I let go just this once and take what I wanted?

Luke's mouth pinched before he nodded his head. "I understand your uncertainty. Our past encounters haven't shown me in a positive light. And for you to let go and trust I won't demean or hurt you, must be hard." His hand rubbed gentle circles over my fist clenched in his shirt. His gaze was sincere as he spoke and he genuinely seemed to get why I'd be worried.

"I'm sorry for behaving like a dick. It was pointed out to me recently that unless I took my head out of my arse, nobody was ever going to want to be with me."

He sighed, his eyes taking on a distant look that said he was no longer thinking about me, but of something else upsetting. A need to reassure him rose and before I could stop myself, I let go of the death grip I had on his shirt and cupped his face. "Why do you act like a knob?"

His brow rose and for a second I worried I might have crossed a line, until a gleam of humour lit his eyes. "Well put. I was acting like a knob," he chuckled. "I had all these ideals hammered into me as a young man." He held up his hand when I went to speak. "Let me finish, please."

Seeing what looked like distress replace the humour, I shut my mouth and waited to hear him out.

"My father loved me, but when I came out to my parents, something changed. I can't say he didn't stop loving me, but I don't think he liked me anymore. He started to drum it into me that if I was into men, then there was an expectation that they would be similar to be. Macho, larger men, that did not look in the least bit effeminate."

He sighed and rubbed at his face before continuing. "The first time I brought home a date, he was the exact opposite of what my father wanted. Let's just say the bruises I got after that date took weeks to heal." The shrug he gave said it didn't matter, but the betrayal on his face was a different matter altogether. "So after that, I started to date men more in line with what my father wanted. Not that I wanted to, it just seemed easier and I wanted him to accept me more than anything."

His eyes misted with tears and the utter dejection in his voice caused a ball of tears to gather in my own throat. I hurt for the man who just wanted his father to accept him. For the denial of a side of him that, if it was like mine, was as fundamental as breathing.

I brought my lips to his, offering a soft kiss of support. A kiss that was only meant to show that I understood that life was sometimes harder than it needed to be. But somehow the kiss changed into something more, his mouth claiming mine. His firm lips opened, his tongue touching the seam of my lips, seeking entry.

With a moan, I opened up for him, need driving any thoughts from my head. My senses swam with his unique flavour. His tongue commandeered mine as it swept against it in a heated caress. My mouth clung to his as he deepened the kiss. I mewled into his mouth as he overwhelmed me.

Gasping for air, my chest heaved but I was reluctant to give up any part of what was happening to me. The world around me faded to nothing except the man holding me and the whirlpool of emotions rushing through my body. My cock strained against the lacy fabric of my underwear, leaking pre-cum with each sweep of his moist tongue against mine. I surrendered, unable to do anything other than hold on for the ride.

Air touched my cheeks and brought me back to my senses, I whined as Luke pulled back, gasping. "Sweet boy, give me a second or else you're going to be naked and impaled on my cock," he ground out through his clenched jaw.

The very idea that Luke was struggling to control himself, gave me ideas of how to cope with being trapped in a box for hours. *Don't think about the box, that's not going to help.* The wave of panic wanted to take away the heady feeling Luke's kiss left in its wake.

I clutched at Luke's face and implored, "Distract me, please?" I licked my lips and lowered my eyelashes, imploring him to give in to me. "Please Daddy, I'll be a good boy and do whatever you want."

Knowing I was playing with fire acting in this way, I couldn't find it in me to care, when I knew that hours trapped in a box doing nothing would make me go out of my mind.

"Are you trying to manipulate… Daddy?" I squirmed and let go of his face, only to find my hands captured. "Answer me. I need you to talk to me so I don't misinterpret what is going on." The break from domineering Daddy pulled me back to my senses.

This was only a game, a hook-up from an app. I needed to remember that, whatever the feelings swimming around inside me were, they were mine, and mine alone.

My pulse danced at what I was about to suggest, but I was in too deep and I didn't want to stop now. "I thought we could keep our date…see how things go, and then maybe if we liked it, we could do it again?" I rushed to speak, needing to get it out without him realising how much I wanted this to extend past one date.

I knew it was ridiculous, but having been shown a glimpse into Luke's past, it kind of explained why I might have been drawn to him, even when he'd not been nice to me. His fight against the integral part of who he was, was not something I'd wish on anyone. My own battle with what I liked wasn't nearly as long and it was only against myself. I couldn't imagine what Luke had dealt with in his past, but I wanted to give him the opportunity to experience what it was like to embrace his inner Daddy.

You're not going to reap the rewards? Oh shut up.

I waited for Luke to answer, ignoring my snarky inner self pointing out the obvious. The seconds felt like an eternity before he responded and the air burst out of my lungs.

"Yes. I'd like to keep our date and see if there could be more between us."

Chapter 8

LUKE

The worry I'm sure Scott wasn't aware he was projecting, slammed into me. He really wanted to continue with the date. With my chest heaving, I attempted to keep my shock to myself, or I prayed I was. My hands wanted to tremble and I did my best to keep them still. Scott's level of vulnerability was doing a number on me, and I could freely admit that all the times I'd been awful to him were about the fact I wanted him. It felt as if the months of yearning I'd secretly done were about to become a thing of the past.

He was offering me the opportunity to fulfil some of my dreams and I was desperate to get started. Then his face scrunched up and he jerked as if he'd been hit by something.

"Shit, your boyfriend." He scrambled to get off my lap and stood on unsteady legs. His finger jabbing in my face, "I don't do cheaters. Shit, how had I forgotten about Brody? Fuck!" He yanked at his hair, his top riding up and flashing a tiny piece of black lace.

The air in the lift seemed to disappear and I wasn't sure if it was from the accusation and distress on Scott's face or the thought of what was under the top he wore. Had he dressed up for me? The very idea derailed my thoughts.

"Are you going to explain yourself? Because this ain't going any further. I knew this was a mistake. I should never have downloaded that bloody app." The rant continued as Scott stood, his body vibrating.

Slowly getting up, my backside complaining about being sat on the hard floor, I crowded Scott, making sure I had his full attention. "Firstly, I am going to spank you for jumping to conclusions, right after we clear this up. I'm single and have been for months now. Brody moved to the Isle of Man to be with his new partner."

The painful memory of Brody and Nick's recent visit left a bitter taste in my mouth. I was happy for my ex now I'd done some soul searching. My behaviour was less than stellar and I wasn't ever going to be able to make up for some of my actions, but at least his visit allowed me to see past the hate. Hate that really should have been directed at the person it belonged to:

me. The self-loathing I'd been left with was a bitter pill to swallow.

Every day since then, I worked on trying to be a better person. Though Rome wasn't built in a day and I needed constant reminders that it was okay to be me and show who I was.

The gleam of need in Scott's eyes pulled me from my own internal battles. Now was not the time to debate if I was able to make myself into a better man. What I needed to do was show Scott that I could be a better man, and accept my mistakes.

"Does that clear up your worries about my single status?"

His quick nod and quivering lip settled my churning gut.

"Do you still feel this is a mistake? I'm not going to take this any further if that's how you feel. We need to both want this, Scott, and until I'm sure we do, nothing is going to happen between us." I held my breath, waiting to see what he'd say to my ultimatum. I didn't have to wait long.

"I want this more than anything, this chance to be your boy, if only for a few hours. But I don't want to be someone's secret. I'm not good at pretending and if you'd come into the restaurant with Brody I don't know how I'd have coped." He shrugged, his face revealing his vulnerability to me.

His words stabbed at my heart when he'd mentioned this only lasting a couple of hours. Did I want more?

The Daddy side of my personality roared to life answering the question. I lifted Scott up so he was eye level. "Once we start this scene, you'll be my boy, no questions asked. You will do as you're told and follow my instructions, understood?" His dilated pupils and the desire I could easily read on his face answered my questions, but I waited for him to reply.

His brow pinched for a moment, "I thought we'd already started Daddy." A shy smile lit his face as he lowered his gaze in submission. My heart leapt in my chest and made it nearly impossible to keep myself in check.

I lowered Scott to the floor and took a step back, my foot catching the bag I'd forgotten about. Glancing down, I kept the devilish thoughts running through my head to myself for the moment.

With the decision made, I went to pick up the bag and then my eyes travelled to Scott's. I stood back up, other ideas crowding my mind. "I think it's time for your punishment. Strip off your top and jeans."

His sharp inhale and his gaze lifting to mine left me struggling to hold on to my control. When he hesitated, I lowered my voice. "Do as Daddy says, or else I will need to find you another punishment."

The speed at which his hands moved to unzip his jeans would have been funny, if not for the sexual tension gripping me by the balls. My cock strained against the fabric of my trousers. My free hand dropped to try and find a more comfortable position, only it didn't get a chance to do more than touch my throbbing erection before Scott's jeans opened to reveal the black silk and lace underwear beneath.

Swallowing became impossible, the saliva in my mouth deserted me, much the same as the blood in my head. A wave of dizziness swept through me at the delicious sight before me. When Scott stepped out of his shoes, and then his trousers, to reveal his pale tattooed legs and sexy underwear, I lost the ability to speak.

My brain was scrambled. I'd no clue he had so much body art. His thighs were covered in intricate black patterns that encircled his whole leg. The pale skin made the tattoos stand out. The silky piece of material barely containing his straining cock added to the overall effect.

He was stunning. The air trapped in my lungs whooshed out as his arms lifted and he peeled off his top to show off the matching lacy top stretched over his slim torso. My thighs quivered and I locked my legs together. The urge to come struck lightning-fast and my hand squeezed my achingly hard cock to stave off the desperate need.

"You're stunning. Fuck! Look at you." My husky words received a sultry smile as Scott dropped his top to the ground and stood tall under my inspection.

His glazed expression and heaving chest showed he was as excited to show himself off as I was to see him like this. Never in my wildest dreams did I imagine this. I wasn't even sure, when he'd mentioned the underwear and sent me the picture, it would have this effect on me in person.

I didn't like it, fuck, that was such an insipid word for what I was feeling. I loved how he looked. Everything about him appealed, the underwear, the pale skin, fuck, even the tattoos, something I'd always considered crass, made him stunning to me.

"Turn around, let me see all of you." The rasped demand was all it took for Scott to slowly pivot after stepping away from his clothes. His small bottom was a perfect handful. The pert cheeks called for me to take a bite, especially encased in the black lacy silk.

"Why did you pick that outfit?"

He slowly turned around, a level of uncertainty in his eyes as they moved to meet mine. "I… I wanted to please you… and…" His breathy response halted, his hands fidgeting at his sides.

"You can tell me, I won't judge you for your choices. And just an FYI, the moment you took off your clothes I had to stop myself from coming in my trousers like some pubescent teenager." I kept going, pretending my flushed cheeks were from the heat of the lift and not embarrassment at my confession. "That never happened to me, even when I was a teenager."

I chuckled at how he squirmed and his cock attempted to peak past the band of his lacy pants.

"You like that Daddy is struggling." It wasn't so much a question, more of a statement, but he nodded, his eyes gleaming as he licked his lush lips and his gaze lowered to my crotch.

Not wanting to let him get away without answering my question, I spoke using a domineering tone. "You didn't finish answering my question. Why did you pick that particular outfit?"

A pink hue covered his cheeks and his eyes flickered to mine then away.

Oh that would not do.

"Eyes on me, sweet boy." As I spoke, I stepped into him. Smelling his arousal, I lowered my mouth to his ear and whispered, "That's another punishment. If I remember correctly we must be up to six now." My fingers trailed down his chest, feeling the soft lace under my fingertips. I stopped over his nipple and slowly drew my nail over the bud until it peaked out further. Plucking it between my fingers I tweaked it hard enough to make him moan and his hips to jerk forward. "Now tell Daddy about this outfit."

His body quivered as he attempted to keep still. "I bought it when you mentioned you liked black when we were messaging."

He gasped as I rewarded him for his honesty. I tugged on his nipple before I licked a path from his ear to his mouth. "Oh you remembered that did you? And you went out to buy something to please your Daddy? Now that deserves a reward." I nibbled at the corner of his parted lips, teasing him. "What reward would you like Daddy to give you?" I know what I wanted, fuck, I wanted everything, I wanted to devour him whole.

"Kiss me again, Daddy, please."

His head moved, his lips already seeking mine. I let him take control for a moment and initiate the kiss. But the moment he opened to me, I seized back control and cupped his face to hold him captive while I devoured his sweet mouth. The moans and whimpers filling my mouth left me needy in ways I'd never felt before. In my past relationships I'd switched, my preference to top was put aside when I picked dominant men. With the knowledge I could let go and be me, I embraced the side I'd kept hidden most of my life.

Controlling Scott, I only released his mouth when his body melted against mine in surrender.

He panted as I released his lips, "Please, Daddy, don't stop."

"Oh, don't fear, I'm not going to stop sweet boy, but I promised you a spanking and I don't break my promises."

Chapter 9

Scott

The gleam in Luke's eyes warned of what was to come. I wasn't sure who was more excited at the prospect of the spanking, me or him. My head quirked to the side when the bag he'd brought with him became his focus again.

What the hell did have in the bag?

I didn't have to wait long to find out when he pulled out a small black butt plug, lube and if I wasn't mistaken, a cock ring. Shit, he'd come prepared. My arse clenched as my cock throbbed at the idea of being denied an orgasm.

His hands full, he gave me a wicked smile that I felt all the way down to the tip of my leaking cock.

"Let's get you situated first, then Daddy can spank his naughty boy."

My mouth opened then shut, the words dying when Luke shook his head. The look was very clear, do not ask questions. I kept them to myself for now and waited to see what he was going to do.

The floor under my feet shifted and I was suddenly reminded of where we were. My chest seized as the air that wanted out refused to leave my lungs. I wrapped my arms around my chest, my eyes now on the door. Was the lift going to plummet to the ground?

"Whatever is going on inside that pretty head of yours?"

The anxiousness I could hear brought my gaze back to Luke. "Is this lift safe? It doesn't feel safe the way it keeps moving." Then it suddenly dawned on me that if something did happen, they'd find me dressed in silk and lace underwear. The colour drained from my face. What would my parents think?

Oh no, don't even think about that.

My arousal wilted at the very idea of my parents having to identify me, dressed in my sexy underwear.

"This lift is perfectly safe, I promise. Look at me, sweet boy. Now."

The command pulled me from my panicked thoughts and I blurted out, "What if we end up squished and my parents have to come and identify my body?" On speaking my fear, my gaze dropped and I went to bend and grab my clothes. My hands shook, then froze.

"Don't even think about putting your clothes back on." The husky growl brought my cock back to life, even when I wanted to curse.

"Daddyyy... I'm scared!" I blinked back the tears that wanted to spill. My emotions were all over the place. I was starting to think it would have been safer to have made a date with a roller coaster, even though I was terrified of those too. At least I knew that would have ended in a few minutes, this torture was going to last for hours.

What did I say about mentioning that? I found myself having an internal argument, that was interrupted when a hand took hold of my chin and tugged on it.

"I know you're scared. But listen to Daddy and hear what I'm saying. I will not let anything bad happen to you. This lift is safe. It's temperamental, a bit like you. But all it needs is a little TLC and it will be working perfectly. I'm also thinking all you need is a little TLC and we'll have you back to normal too."

A watery chuckle escaped as Luke kept his gaze fixed on me. The truth shone out of his eyes, and though I didn't know him well enough to know if the trust I felt was real, I went with it. I gave him a nod. "Okay, Daddy. I'll try not to let it worry me."

His brow rose and a mischievous twinkle came to life in his gaze. "Oh, that won't do. Now you've challenged me to make you forget all about your worries." The wolfish smile gave me goosebumps all over my body as he released my chin. "Now, where was I?"

I glanced at the large hand still holding the butt plug, packets of lube and cock ring. His gaze followed mine and the twinkling light in his eyes increased. "Yes, now I remember," he chuckled evilly.

Like he'd forgotten, yeah right.

I knew fine well he'd forgotten nothing, but I wasn't stupid enough to point that out.

The slight shift of the floor again made my pulse spike, that was until Daddy lowered himself to the floor. He placed the things he'd been holding next to him, then removed his suit jacket and tie. He spread his thighs and patted his leg, "Come here and lay face down over my lap."

Kneeling down on the floor, I sucked my lower lip between my teeth, working on figuring out how to do what Luke wanted without my head jamming up against the opposite wall. It was only then that I really noticed how tight the space was. It took all my willpower not to let the thought take hold as I stretched across his legs. Wiggling so that my cock was not trapped against his thigh but between his legs, I placed my forearms on the floor and lay my head on them and brought my knees in close to his thigh.

A low groan followed the move and I lifted my bottom up, impatient to get started. It had been years since I'd felt the heat burning through my body from a good spanking and my belly danced with excitement.

Warm skin touched my lacy covered bottom, slowly caressing the material. I shivered as the gentleness of the touch ramped up my desire, knowing it wouldn't remain so gentle for long. My eyelids grew heavy as large hands continued to explore my body. I groaned at the feel of Luke's strong hands massaging my tense muscles.

"Your body is beautiful," Luke said, his voice several octaves lower.

The sexy tone made it difficult for me to keep still. My cock thrummed and I could see I'd made an error having it hang between Luke's thighs. It left me with nothing to gain any friction against, with the exception of my panties. I groaned when he continued to torture me with caresses.

It seemed to last an eternity before he slipped my underwear down. "Lift up your hips."

The growl brooked no argument, not that I wanted to. I was more than happy to get to the next stage, whatever that was going to be. Once he'd removed the scrap of lacy fabric, he spread my legs wider. His hand lowered between my thighs and took hold of my cock, stroking me firmly.

Clenching my eyes shut, I panted and groaned, thrusting into his warm, firm grip. The next thing I felt was the sharp sting as a slap rang out. I yelped, before I shifted my hips, wanting more as heat spread over my arse cheek. Sensations flooded through my body at the next slap and the following, his other hand continuing to stroke me in time to the spankings.

Slap, stroke, slap, stroke, the rhythm pulled me into a world of pleasure. My mind clouded as the desire took control, any worries I'd had dissolved under the onslaught of the licks of pleasure curling inside my body and spreading out to engulf me. I felt electrified, my body writhed. My thighs strained to stay open as a fine layer of sweat coated my skin.

My orgasm rose hard and fast at the sounds of flesh hitting flesh and the feel of Daddy's hand sliding over my rock hard cock, milking me.

"Daddyyyyyyy… I'mmm… coming!" I wailed and found myself panting and wanting to cry in distress when the hands immediately stopped and left my body.

Daddy growled, "You will not come until I tell you to."

It was too much in my heightened state, my thighs strained to close as I panted through the urge to not come and do as I was told. But it was damn hard with him being all growly. My cock was not getting the message as it bucked into the air, seeking anything to make it come.

I whined, not sure which way was up with my cock taking charge.

Firm fingers took hold of my sac and squeezed until the pain made them throb and the urge to come subsided. Once I could see straight I lifted my head off my shaky arms. "You did that on purpose," I complained half-heartedly.

Luke shrugged and chuckled. "Of course I did, what kind of Daddy would I be if I didn't give my boy exactly what he wanted?"

I wanted to grumble that it wasn't what I wanted, but that would be a complete lie. I didn't bother, instead laying my head back on my arms and prayed Luke would keep going, because I hadn't had nearly enough.

Chapter 10

Luke

When Scott lay his head back down, I let loose the goofy grin I'd struggled to contain when he'd pouted at me. I'd been tempted for a moment to let him come, but then I realised we'd still be here for a long time yet. And as much as I wanted to watch him fall apart, I also wanted to make sure the panic that kept crossing his face when he remembered where we were, was the last thing on his mind.

To that end, I stopped. I thought of the leather cock ring I'd bought with me, wondering if I could see how long he could hold out before he begged to come. I picked up the soft leather. "Lift up your hips sweet boy." The endearment rolled off my tongue. I'd learned long ago of his sweet tooth, so to my mind, the term suited him. He really was a sweet boy, and because he didn't question it and his eyes lit up every time I used it, it'd stuck.

The hips on my lap shifted and rose up. The now crimson skin shone under the lights and filled me with a sense of deep-seated satisfaction. That Scott wanted this as much as I wanted to give it to him left me swimming in a pool of emotions so deep I wasn't sure I wouldn't drown before I could find my feet again.

Not wanting to examine them too closely, I took hold of the cock hanging heavy between his thighs. I slowly slid the soft leather up his shaft. A needy whimper and hip swivel was followed by a long drawn out moan as I slowly tightened the leather until it fitted snugly against the base of his hairless cock. I scraped my nail over the tip of his leaking slit before rubbing gentle circles over the sticky head.

"Ohhhhh! Daddyyyy! More, I need more, givememore," he groaned out on a rush, his hips pushing back and down in quick succession as he writhed and strained against me.

"What does my boy need? Tell Daddy," I ground out through a clenched jaw. This open display of need was driving my own desire to a level that was making it hard to keep control. Had I ever been like this before?

Desperate and needy, his behaviour clawed at my control. It ripped it away leaving me nothing more than an animal that wanted to mount Scott and fuck him hard. Mark him as mine and make sure he understood what this really meant.

Shaken to my very core at how violent my emotions were and by how much I was struggling to not express them, my hands trembled as I removed them, not convinced I could keep my touch gentle.

I picked up the lube with trembling fingers and ripped open the packet with my teeth as I lifted the small ribbed butt plug. Slicking it was lube, I dropped the package.

My attention returned to the bottom that continued to quiver on my thighs. I shifted, opening my legs to give Scott a more secure base before I nudged his thighs further apart. "Tilt your hips for Daddy."

He groaned but did as he was told, his face remaining buried in his arms. The small movement shoved his bottom up and gave me the first glimpse of his pale pink pucker. I took the fingers covered in lube and slowly teased the wrinkled flesh. Scott gasped and stopped moving as I slowly slid the tip of my slick finger into his channel. The tightness was almost unbearable as his sheath latched onto my finger.

With my cock valiantly digging against the zip of my trousers, searching for a way to find its way into the tight sheath, I sucked in a breath. I strained to hold still and allow Scott the time he needed to relax. Then I had a sudden thought that derailed everything.

I blurted out, "You're not a virgin, are you?"

The very idea that his first time was going to be in a lift, left me cold.

His head lifted and his flushed face turned to me. His glazed, heavy-lidded eyes did a number on me, and I struggled to comprehend what he was saying for a second.

"No Daddy… it's… just been a really long time." With that his head sunk back onto his arms. There was a flash of embarrassment on his face before he hid from me.

"Boy, look at me." I wanted him to see my face when I spoke. I didn't want there to be any misunderstanding between us. He needed to see how much this pleased me, no matter how much it shouldn't.

When his head lifted, albeit a little reluctantly, I rewarded him by pushing my finger a little deeper inside him, searching out his prostate. Once I found it, I slowly teased the small raised nub of flesh. His eyes clouded with lust and his mouth opened and stayed that way as he moaned and humped my hand, trying to get me to repeat the move.

"Look at me."

Eyes that had closed slowly drifted open to half-mast.

"I can't tell you how happy I am that you haven't been with anyone for a long time. I know that makes me a selfish bastard, but I want you to know it pleases Daddy." To stress my point, I teased him further, before sinking my finger deeper. Then I fucked him slowly with my finger until he could take me effortlessly.

I withdrew, replacing one finger with two until I felt he was ready to take the plug. Only then did I reluctantly leave his tight channel and press the tip of the butt plug against his slick pucker.

Scott buried his head back down in his arms, the whimpers turning to pleading as I teased his rim before relenting and slowly easing the plug in until the end was flush against his cheeks.

I chuckled at what was going to happen next. I flicked the button on the tip just as Scott's body relaxed against my thighs. His loud wail of, "Ohhhhhh, fuckkkk!" when the plug started to vibrate against his prostate, turned my chuckle into flown blown laughter.

He grunted around several pants. "That's not funny," he said as his arse undulated.

"Oh boy, look at you. You look fucking spectacular seeking out your pleasure for Daddy."

His complaints died and his body stopped moving as his head came up, his gaze meeting mine. The air remained trapped in my chest at the look of adoration. "I'd do anything for my Daddy," he said breathlessly.

Those words hit me dead centre in my chest. I could feel the impact as my body jerked, and my cock leaked. The desire to be his Daddy for more than this one encounter left me trying to reel my feelings back in.

My mouth opened and out poured the truth, regardless of whether I was ready to face it or not. "I want nothing more than to be your Daddy." My lips flapped open, I wasn't sure which of us was more shocked by the truth in what I'd said.

I gulped when Scott's eyes sheened with tears and the look of adoration became something akin to devotion. I was glad I was sat down because I wasn't sure in that moment if I could have remained standing. The vulnerability cut at the barriers I'd used for years to keep people from seeing the real me.

"I'd like that, Daddy," he whispered, bewitching me when his eyes lowered and his bottom lifted up, asking for what he wanted. Unable to deny either of us, I ignored the emotions surging through me and raised my hand. The first spanking received a mewl and a bum wiggle.

"You wouldn't be trying to rush Daddy now would you?" I growled for effect, not missing the full-body shiver as his hips lifted. "Such a naughty boy." Not waiting for him to respond, I gave him several hard stinging slaps, over the whole of his buttocks. The sound of the slaps merged with the buzzing of the plug and Scott's moans and whimpers.

Sweat coated his body as he strained and ground uselessly against me. His cock hung heavy between my thighs, not able to gain any friction to relieve the ache that had to be growing.

When the mewls increased to obscure words, I parted his cheeks and eased the plug out an inch before shoving it back in hard. Repeating the move, Scott's back arched and he lifted up on to his knees. "Oh no more... fuck me... fuck me... fuck...meeeeee!" he wailed, his head thrown back, his hips thrusting in desperation.

The sight took my breath away, the very idea of not giving him what he wanted, was inconceivable. "Anything, boy." I shifted him so I could pull my legs from under him and was met with whining.

"Now Daddy... now!"

I growled at the cheeky demand, but I couldn't hold off any longer under such need. I stood up on trembling legs and quickly removed my remaining clothes, taking the condom from my pocket that I'd placed there earlier.

I knelt behind Scott and rolled on the condom, my gaze sweeping the floor for one of the packets of lube. Scott impatiently waved his red backside in my direction. I shook my head, he really needed to be taken in hand, but I was past that stage of delaying any longer.

Once I'd lubed my cock, I removed the plug and smeared more lube over his clenching pucker. I sank my finger deep, the tight sheath relinquished my finger faster than the first time, though he was still so tight.

How the fuck was I going to keep control when I sank into the hot, tight channel? I had no clue, but I fucking hoped I had enough willpower to allow Scott the time to adjust. I sucked in several breaths while I stretched him.

"Enough, I'm ready...I am... Daddy... please!" Scott cried out. Sweat soaked his hair and stuck to his flushed face as he turned his head towards me. His molten eyes begged me to give him what he wanted.

Unable to fight the need any longer, I withdrew my fingers and prayed to the heavens I could go slow. The heat of his flesh seemed to sear the tip of my cock as I pushed against his rim. It resisted for a moment before relaxing enough for me to push past the tight ring of muscle. My eyes were surely crossing at the unbearable squeeze that left my cock strangled. Undecided if it was heaven or pure hell, I panted as sweat slid down my face as I held still, willing Scott's body to relax and release me enough that I was able to breathe again.

My chest heaved and my lungs felt as if they were going to burst by the time his body relaxed enough to allow me to sink in another inch. By the time I was fully seated inside him, I wasn't sure I was going to embarrass myself and come after only two seconds. I squeezed my butt cheeks and strained to keep my orgasm from pouring from my throbbing cock.

"Daddyyyyy move!"

The whine said in a sulky tone was too much, I slid my hand under Scott while I still had the brainpower to fumble and unlace the cock ring. Once it fell to the floor, I eased back and gave Scott what he demanded. I tilted his hips to make sure I hit his prostate, and then I slammed into him.

He wailed and his back arched as I didn't give him a chance to do more, and set up a furious pace. The sound of flesh hitting flesh filled the small space, ringing loudly in my ears.

My vision tunnelled down to one thing, my boy's pleasure.

I moved over him, caging my arms around him as I buried my face in his neck and inhaled the scent of aftershave and sweaty musk. My body taking over, my cock drove relentlessly into his clenching arse. He bore down, his channel tightening and strangling my cock painfully. He screamed and his body juddered uncontrollably. I reached under him and took hold of his throbbing cock, milking his orgasm from him.

His cock pulsed in my hand and his channel clasped me so tightly, pulling cum straight from my cock. I ground against his warm backside. "Your mine now. Do you hear me? Mine," I ground out through clenched teeth, mindless to all but what was happening between us.

The returning moan and his hips jerking as his channel pulsed repeatedly said his cock liked that idea, as it continued to spurt cum onto the floor beneath him. The moment seemed endless as we took pleasure from each other until Scott's body started to shake with the effort of holding my weight against his sweaty back.

Easing off him, I slid out of his body and instantly felt bereft. The needy whine Scott released matched my sentiments. I rubbed at his sweaty skin, "I need to move sweet boy, or I'm going to crush you."

Chapter 11

Scott

As Luke shifted his cock slid from my body, I felt the loss so acutely I bit my lip to stop from demanding he put it back. When he'd finally quit teasing me and pushed inside me, I'd lost my mind. My sense of self seemed to meld with Luke's as if he'd taken away all my doubts and worries about my life in general and replaced them with nothing but joy. He surrounded me, making me feel that I mattered more than anything else in the world.

You are not his world, and he isn't yours.

The voice wouldn't quiet and I desperately wanted to tell it to fuck off, but I knew that no matter how much I wanted this to be more, it just wasn't. There was no way Luke meant the things he'd said. They had to have been spoken in the heat of the moment, right?

Huffing out a frustrated sigh, I found myself pulled against a sweaty bare chest. I let Luke tug me into his lap as he sat back onto the floor, his chest rising rapidly and his heart beating fast against me.

I nestled my head into the crook of his neck once he shifted me so my legs were stretched out to the side, then his arm wrapped around my back and held me tightly to him. I lay sleepily against him, my thoughts continuing to try and take away my happy orgasmic bliss.

"You're a loud thinker. Stop worrying. I meant everything I said. It wasn't the heat of the moment. I want more from you than just this one time."

His reassurances let my heart rate decrease and stopped my ears from buzzing. I relaxed against him fully and let him hold me the way I craved. He rocked me gently, his lips brushed the top of my sweaty hair before his chin came to rest on top of my head.

A smile spread over my face at the contented sigh that rumbled up Luke's chest. My eyes drifted closed with my body too tired to fight against sleep.

I could worry about what it all meant later. The movement of Luke's chest rising and falling lulled me to sleep.

***

My eyes fluttered open and for a moment I couldn't figure out where the hell I was. I blinked and then it all came flooding back when the arms holding me shifted and tightened around me. I nestled back into Luke's warm embrace, uncertain what had woken me. Idly, I wondered how long we'd been stuck. The panic that would typically accompany that thought didn't materialise and I found myself grinning stupidly at the wall.

A scratching sound came from above my head and caught my attention. I lifted my head and Luke muttered something but didn't wake. I shifted my eyes up to the ceiling, blinking, unsure if what I was seeing was real or my imagination. The tiles in the roof seemed to be moving. That can't be right?

When it moved again, it registered past my sleepy brain that someone was not only outside the lift, but on top of the roof. *Oh fuck.*

I didn't think. I scrambled off Luke, jerking him awake.

"What... what is it?"

He blinked sleepily up at me as I stood, unsure what I should do first. My gaze swept the floor. What we'd done was evident in the dried cum, discarded butt plug, condom and lube packets scattered on the floor. Never mind the fact we were both naked, with the exception of my lacy top.

"There's someone on the roof of the lift," I hissed, my hand pointing to the tiles that were still moving.

A look of alarm filled Luke's face as he jerked and them jumped up. He grabbed frantically for my clothes first and shoved them at me. I stood still, my hands hung uselessly at my sides. His first thought was about *me*.

My eyes filled with tears even as he frantically whispered, "Get dressed. I don't want anyone seeing you looking like that."

He didn't say he didn't want anyone seeing what we'd done. No, he'd expressly said 'me'. I forgot about the clothes he'd shoved at me and stood on my tiptoes and gave him a kiss. "Okay, Daddy."

He stilled, his eyes filling with emotions that made my chest hurt before he lowered his gaze and shielded them from me. I wanted to demand he be open with me, but the movement now was accompanied by increasing noises. So I took the clothes and started to dress frantically, praying we managed to get sorted before whoever was above us managed to get the lift moving.

With Luke picking up the discarded wrappers and butt plug, I averted my face to hide the heat colouring my cheeks. *A bit late for that, you should be embarrassed by the way you begged for his cock. Surely that should be more reason for being self-conscious.*

I shifted, my cock twitched not getting with the programme we were about to be set free, when Luke collected the plug and my rampant thoughts reminded me how good it had felt.

Once Luke shoved everything back into the bag, I checked the floor, using my trainer to try and remove the cum. I sniffed the air. Shit, there was no getting away from the scent of sex in the small box. There was no window or door to open. I shrugged, we couldn't have everything, could we?

The sound of loud clanging was followed by the whole lift shifting under my feet. The thoughts from earlier, about how I wasn't panicking anymore, fled under my hammering heart, now fighting with my sternum to escape. My gaze flew to Luke who instantly dropped the bag and held open his arms. I all but launched myself into them.

The minute his arms wrapped around me, I relaxed. The ease with which he offered comfort stole my breath and made me fall even harder for him. His arms gave me a sense of security I'd never experienced before and only made me worry more about what would happen the minute we were freed from the lift.

It dawned on me that I was no longer worried about being trapped, but more about how Luke would act once we'd left the cocoon we'd been hiding in. The lift had somehow offered us both the space to let go and embrace the possibilities. Would that change when we were free?

The lift jerked once more, only this time the doors opened a fraction. A grimy, sweaty face poked through the hole. "Luke, we should have you free in about two minutes, Dave is just changing the part that got jammed." When the guy's nose started to twitch and his eyes widened, I buried my face in Luke's broad chest. When he didn't try to push me away but kept right on holding me, I sighed. Oh I was in so deep I could no longer see the wood for the trees.

"That's fine Bob. We'll be okay for a few more minutes. Scott's a little scared of confined spaces, but we somehow managed to stop him from freaking out." His warm fingers lifted my chin up. "Didn't we?" He winked before lowering his mouth to my ear and whispering, "Sweet boy."

My cock recalled how much it liked to be Luke's sweet boy and firmed faster than I could get my head to catch up. I pleaded with my eyes that he stop, before everyone could see just how we'd entertained ourselves.

I nodded, finding myself unable to speak past the ball stuck in my throat.

"Erm... well... yes. We should have you out in a jiffy." With that Bob head disappeared and the doors shut again.

"What did you say that for?" I whined and glared up at him.

"Because I knew it would distract you and stop you worrying. Things will be fine, you'll see." Luke tweaked my nose before kissing its tip as the lift started to move and then stop. The doors opened and Luke eased away from me.

I wanted to cry out at how cold I felt with him leaving me, but the mechanic eyeing me, whose nose was still twitching, made me think better of it. I stepped out of the lift on shaky legs and put a little distance between us.

Not paying any attention to the conversation going on between Luke and who I now figured must be Bob, I stood fretting.

What happens now? Do we go to the hotel room, or should I go home?

I checked my wrist and my eyes widened. Fuck, we'd been in there seven hours. The thought registered with my bladder and I suddenly needed to pee really badly. My feet shifted and my eyes searched the corridor for restrooms. I knew some hotels had them in the hallways and I really hoped Luke's did.

A sign halfway down the corridor called to me. Not wanting to wait on the chance they'd stop anytime soon, I all but ran down the carpeted hallway. Not sure either man noticed as neither was paying me any attention.

The door was like a beacon calling to my overfull bladder that wanted to let out the pee. It wanted out now and it wasn't up to stopping for anything or anyone. Bursting through the door of the elegant bathroom, I jogged to the toilet, slamming the door behind me. I hopped about while trying to quickly fumble with my zip.

The level of desperation was creeping past my limits on holding in the pee. The second the air hit my cock it was all over. I had the foresight to jerk it over the toilet and thanked the lord it didn't hit anywhere but the bowl. With a sigh I spent the next thirty seconds feeling the relief that only comes after you'd held off peeing until your eyes crossed.

I kept my eyes off the dried cum flaking to the floor and waited out my bladder emptying. Once finished I zipped up, washed my hands and headed back into the corridor. My eyes moved to where I'd left Luke not more than a few minutes earlier. A sob rose in my throat at the now empty hallway.

He left me! He left me!

The thought on repeat, I sucked in the sobs and wiped at my eyes as I went to the door highlighted with a sign to show it was the stairs, dragging my feet down the nine flights.

My heart heavy, I popped my head out the door marked exit, seeing no one near. I stepped out and worked on stopping myself from running. Instead I took my time, not making eye contact with anyone. Once outside, I noticed the guy from earlier was nowhere in sight and I thanked my lucky stars. I wasn't sure I could hold myself together if he'd stopped to question if I'd found my friend. Fuck, I'd found so much more than that. Leaving the hotel behind me, I walked down the street before hailing a taxi.

When a taxi stopped, I climbed in and let out the sobs that had been choking me.

"Hey mate, you ok?"

The alarm in the guy's voice kept me from blustering out my woes.

"I'm fine," I said, giving him my address and pretending not to notice how he spent more time looking at me in the mirror than on the road.

The feel of my pocket vibrating pulled me from my misery.

DaddyL: *Where the hell are you? This is so not over and don't you think it is. This is only the beginning. And I swear when I get my hands on you, you'll not be able to sit down for a week.*

On a hiccuped sob, my heart soared with relief. Warmth replaced the cold feeling that enveloped me the moment I'd seen the empty corridor.

SassyS: *Yes Daddy... I'm sorry. I'm in a taxi heading home, when I came out of the bathroom you were gone. I thought you'd left and it was over... When do you want to give me my punishment?*

It wasn't over. It wasn't over. Joy burst out of me and I giggled at the feelings spreading over me. Maybe The App was only the beginning for us?

Epilogue

I turned around when Bob stopped waffling about how long it had taken for the part to arrive and then went into a long-winded talk about what was wrong with the lift.

My mouth opened and shut. Where the hell had Scott gone? He'd been there a minute ago I was sure. I grunted at Bob when he went to say something more, waving him off. "Did you see where Scott went?"

His eyes narrowed on me but I kept my gaze steady, working on not showing the panic wanting to choke me.

"No boss, he was there a minute ago. Maybe he just wanted to leave 'cause he'd been trapped so long." He shrugged as if it was nothing.

The urge to shout at him was stifled only by the fear I'd fucked up and given Scott the wrong impression that I didn't want for this to continue. I racked my brains to come up with an answer as to why he'd run off. I muttered to Bob

I'd catch up with him later as I stormed off to the stairs; he had to have gone down them.

Opening the door, I walked to the top and looked down. Seeing no sign of Scott I raced down them, breathless and with my heart squeezing painfully in my chest. I ran into the foyer, my gaze sweeping the reception. Finding nothing, I raced to the door.

Rupert's replacement for the evening, Griffin, stood taller as I came out. "Good evening, Griffin. Have you seen a dark-haired gent dressed in jeans and a black top leave in the last few minutes?"

The head shake set my stomach to jumping. "No sir, I've just returned from helping a couple with their bags. I unfortunately haven't seen a gentleman meeting that description. If I see him would you like me to call you?"

His brows rose and the interest in his eyes stopped me cold. "No, it's fine, thank you." Going back through the door I searched the foyer again, coming up empty. I headed for the lifts cursing with every step.

Why had he run off?

I was going to spank his backside so hard when I found him. Ten minutes later, my anger was past simmering and well on its way to boiling when my search of the hotel room I booked showed Scott had never gone there. It took stepping into the lift to make me consider that maybe that was where he'd gone. Only I was wrong and now I didn't know what I was going to do.

Do I leave it, or do I message him?

Was him leaving his way of saying he didn't want more?

I took several deep breaths and sat on the end of the large king-sized bed I'd never got to use and eyed the floor. *Pull yourself together. He couldn't fake the way he behaved, it was real. He wanted you.*

Was I thinking that because I wanted it to be true? Was it real? Driving myself to distraction, I got up and paced the room, feeling like a caged animal.

No. What we had was real, the connection more profound than a quick fuck. Hell, I'd had plenty of those in the past. This was different. I sighed. *Then what the fuck do I do now?*

I sat back down and took out my phone. I eyed The App before opening it with trembling fingers.

DaddyL: *Where the hell are you? This is so not over and don't you think it is. This is only the beginning. And I swear when I get my hands on you, you'll not be able to sit down for a week.*

The thirty seconds it took for a reply to come through felt like an eternity. My palms sweated as my phone buzzed.

SassyS: *Yes Daddy… I'm sorry. I'm in a taxi heading home, when I came out of the bathroom you were gone. I thought you'd left and it was over… When do you want to give me my punishment?*

The simple explanation finally got my heart to stop feeling like it was no longer whole.

A grin spread over my face as I glanced at the phone.

Oh, my naughty boy was going to pay in the most delicious way. The App might have started this, but I was going to finish it and make Scott mine, no matter what it took.

With that thought running through my head, I started typing.

Finding the perfect Daddy was easy with The App, but would Scott be able to keep him?

Scott Rainsford had been shocked to find that his blind date was someone who he not only knew, but wasn't enamoured with. Now he must decide if one hot encounter can change his opinion of a man he can't stop thinking about.

That is until DaddyL shows what he really wants: Scott.

But nothing is simple. A first time Daddy, interfering friends, and past mistakes create more bumps in the road. Can two men who seem worlds apart, go from enemies to lovers, to more, and find their happiness together?

This is a HEA, MM gay romance with Daddy kink, spanking, lace and silk, and a very naughty boy who loves nothing better than teasing his Daddy.

Warning: This is the follow on from The App: Daddy Kink and the author would recommend reading that book first because these two men were just too complicated for one book.

Prologue

LUKE

I turned around when Bob stopped waffling on about how long it had taken for the part to arrive and then went into a long-winded talk about what was wrong with the lift.

My mouth opened and shut. Where the hell had Scott gone? He'd been there a minute ago, I was sure. I grunted at Bob when he went to say something more, waving him off. "Did you see where Scott went?"

His eyes narrowed on me but I kept my gaze steady, working on not showing the panic wanting to choke me.

"No boss, he was there a minute ago. Maybe he just wanted to leave 'cause he'd been trapped so long." He shrugged as if it was nothing.

The urge to shout at him was stifled only by the fear I'd fucked up and given Scott the impression that I didn't want for this to continue. I racked my brains to come up with an answer as to why he'd run off. I muttered to Bob that I'd catch up with him later as I stormed off to the stairs; he had to have gone down them.

Opening the door, I walked to the top and looked down. Seeing no sign of Scott I raced down them, breathless and with my heart squeezing painfully in my chest. I ran into the foyer, my gaze sweeping the reception. Finding nothing, I raced to the door.

Rupert's replacement for the evening, Griffin, stood taller as I came out. "Good evening, Griffin. Have you seen a dark-haired gent dressed in jeans and a black top leave in the last few minutes?"

The head shake set my stomach to jumping. "No sir, I've just returned from helping a couple with their bags. I unfortunately haven't seen a gentleman meeting that description. If I see him would you like me to call you?"

His brows rose and the interest in his eyes stopped me cold. "No, it's fine, thank you." Going back through the door, I searched the foyer again, coming up empty. I headed for the lifts, cursing with every step.

Why had he run off?

I was going to spank his backside so hard when I found him. Ten minutes later, my anger was past simmering and well on its way to boiling when my search of the hotel room I booked showed Scott had never gone there. It had taken stepping into the lift to make me consider that maybe that was where he'd gone. Only I was wrong and now I didn't know what I was going to do.

Do I leave it, or do I message him?

Was him leaving his way of saying he didn't want more?

I took several deep breaths and sat on the end of the large king-sized bed I'd never got to use and eyed the floor. *Pull yourself together. He couldn't fake the way he behaved, it was real. He wanted you.*

Did I think that because I wanted it to be true? Was it real? Driving myself to distraction, I got up and paced the room, feeling like a caged animal.

No. What we had was real, the connection more profound than a quick fuck. Hell, I'd had plenty of those in the past. This was different. I sighed. *Then what the fuck do I do now?*

I sat back down and took out my phone. I eyed The App before opening it with trembling fingers.

DaddyL: *Where the hell are you? This is so not over and don't you think it is. This is only the beginning. And I swear when I get my hands on you, you'll not be able to sit down for a week.*

The thirty seconds it took for a reply to come through felt like an eternity. My palms sweated as my phone buzzed.

SassyS: *Yes Daddy... I'm sorry. I'm in a taxi heading home. When I came out of the bathroom you were gone. I thought you'd left and it was over... When do you want to give me my punishment?*

The simple explanation finally got my heart to stop feeling like it was no longer whole.

A grin spread over my face as I glanced at the phone.

Oh, my naughty boy was going to pay in the most delicious way. The App might have started this, but I was going to finish it and make Scott mine, no matter what it took.

With that thought running through my head, I started typing.

DaddyL: *When is your next day off?*

In my mind I could already envision Scott coming to my home and what I could do to him without the worry of a broken lift to think about. My hand tightened around the phone when the icon showed he was typing.

SassyS: *We are slammed at work. I've agreed*

to do extra shifts over the next two weeks

With a sinking heart, I read the message twice before sighing.

DaddyL: *Okay…tell me when your next actual day off is. I'll make sure I take the day off.*

Immediately my head started to argue with me. *Why are you promising that? You know that might not be possible.*

Refusing to listen to the voice of reason, I hit send and waited with my heart thundering in my ears.

SassyS: *I'm not sure without looking at the rota at work. I never write it down because I usually just look when I'm in and remember what my next shift is… sorry Daddy. Can I tell you tomorrow?*

The thought that he might be fobbing me off had started to push its way into my subconscious but was doused as I read the last part of the message. *Daddy.* Why did that one word make my heart tremble with need?

With shaking fingers, I typed back.

DaddyL: *Yes, that's fine. But I want you to send me all your designated shifts so I know when you're working.*

An idea formed as I hit send and a smile spread over my lips. There was nothing to say I couldn't see Scott before his day off.

SassyS: *Okay…*

DaddyL: *You wouldn't be rolling your eyes at me, would you?*

SassyS: *Maybe…*

I roared with laughter as I stood up and clutched my phone. God, I was going to be in so much trouble, I could see it now. Tears leaked out of my eyes as I tried to pull myself together so I could leave the room. I was sure my colleagues would think I was having some sort of break down as I very rarely laughed in work.

I had a feeling laughing was going to be something I was going to need to get used to. *And what's wrong with that?*

Absolutely nothing.

The smile was firmly fixed to my face as I left the room, scrolling through my phone to find the number to my favourite restaurant.

Let's see how Scott likes a surprise visit.

Chapter 1

Scott

Spotting Adam talking with Carl as I walked into the restaurant kitchen, I kept my head down. *Oh please don't let him ask me how the date went, please!*

My pleas, it seemed, went unanswered when Adam's head turned in my direction and his gaze narrowed on me. He said something to Carl before he hot-footed it in my direction. Hopes of him not asking about the day before vanished when he spoke.

"Why didn't you answer my text messages? I've been worried sick that some maniac had taken you hostage and wouldn't let you go," he demanded angrily, his face flushed with indignation.

"Keep your bloody voice down will you," I hissed back, taking hold of his arm to drag him into the locker room. I didn't look at the staff milling around who were eyeing us with curiosity. The last thing I wanted was the people

I worked with knowing I'd used a kink app to get a date.

What's wrong with that?

I tried to think of a valid reason why there was something wrong with it as the door shut behind Adam. When I couldn't come up with anything, I glowered at him instead. "I didn't answer your six texts because I needed some time to process, okay? And as you can see, I'm perfectly safe." I huffed and went to my locker. Not sure I was ready to answer the questions about who DaddyL had turned out to be.

All night I'd tossed and turned, recalling what had happened from the moment I'd realised it was the one customer that comes to the restaurant that had the ability to make me cry; Luke Mason.

The underground journey to work this morning had been interesting, as my cock wanted to show all the other commuters where my head was at. The scene in the lift was something I didn't think I'd ever forget. Hell, the fact Luke could make me forget we were stuck in that claustrophobic space was epic in itself given my phobia.

A tug at my arm had me turn and face Adam. I sighed resignedly at his pinched expression and the look of concern in his eyes.

"You're being an arse right now and it's not like you. Tell me what's up? Did something bad happen yesterday? You were so happy two days ago and now I'm not sure what you are," Adam said as he watched me like a hawk.

"Did something happen… yeah, you could say that." I groaned and gave a pitiful tug to pull my arm from his grasp.

The pressure of his grip increased. "Please tell me what's up."

The alarm in his voice had me relenting. "DaddyL is… Luke Mason," I muttered.

Adam's hand fell from my arm as his mouth hung open.

"Yep… that expression right there on your face just about sums it up."

"You're kidding me, right? Those flirty messages were from that grumpy bastard?" His voice had gone up several octaves, which would have been funny if this was a laughing matter.

"No, I'm not," I stated stiffly. I instantly got the impression Adam thought I might not have kept the date, my suspicions were confirmed a second later.

"I bet his face was a picture when you told him where to get off…" his voice trailed off, then his eyebrows rose up his forehead when he scrutinised my face. "You did tell him where to get off, right?"

My gaze lowered and I hunched into my coat as I tried to come up with an answer that didn't result in Adam going off on one. I was never very good with conflict or having to face up to angry people.

"Oh my god... did you get down and dirty with Luke Mason?" he all but shouted, his body vibrating as I peeled my eyes off the floor to look at him.

Seeing no way out, I nodded, my teeth digging into my lower lip. Sparks of anger fired at me from Adam's irate eyes and I braced for the rant that was about to come my way.

"How could you? He's treated you like shit for... forever. The guy has never shown you any consideration and you let him fuck you. Are you demented you fool?"

Heat flooded my face as I listened to his tirade and found I couldn't really argue back. Luke had been a shit to me and had made me cry on more than one occasion.

Yet.

Yesterday he'd shown a side to himself that called to me and was the reason I hadn't slept for shit. How could I, when all I could think about was how he'd behaved in the past without the intensity of the situation getting in the way? The reality of how Luke had acted up until yesterday couldn't be brushed aside in the cold light of day, or in my case, the dark sleepless night.

Then why did he act so caring when you had a breakdown in the lift? Why did he hold you and make you feel protected and safe in ways no one else ever had?

These thoughts were why I couldn't find my balance in all of this. My eyes implored Adam to give me a second when he stood and waited for me to come up with a valid reason.

"The thing is, when I got to the hotel and got into the lift, I still didn't know who my date was with. Luke followed me into the lift, and he figured it out at the same time as me. But it was too late to leave then because the bloody lift broke."

Just mentioning it caused sweat to coat my upper lip. Unable to stand still, I stepped back from Adam and paced in front of him, refusing to look at him as I continued. "I suffer from claustrophobia and, well, I had a bit of a meltdown when the lift broke. Then Luke went all Daddy on me… and fuck, I couldn't get my head to listen to reason, especially when he explained some of the reasons for the way he's behaved." I chanced a quick glance at Adam, but his face was still a mask of disbelief. Without the option of sharing what Luke had told me in confidence, I didn't know how to make him understand.

You don't fully get what happened, so how the hell can you make Adam understand?

I didn't get a chance to say any more as the door behind me opened. I swung around and Sawyer stopped mid-step, his gaze moving between Adam and me. "Should I go and come back? But I have to warn you, I might make a mess on the kitchen floor." He grinned at us as he shifted from foot to foot.

"No, it's fine, go take a leak. I'm not having Carl shout at me today as well," I muttered. Adam gave me a hard stare and a 'we haven't finished this conversation' look as he stepped around Sawyer and walked out the door. His stiff posture was the last thing I saw as the door closed.

Well fuck, that went well.

Not.

Sawyer stood unmoving for a brief moment, a look of concern on his face, and I wondered if I was going to have to explain myself to him too. Breathing a sigh of relief when he walked to the bathroom door, I waited till it shut behind him before I sagged against the wall of lockers.

What the fuck do I do now?

No closer to an answer than I had been all night, I changed my shirt and made sure I was presentable before returning to the kitchen. Trying not to think about the double shift I'd agreed to, I went to check the tables were ready for lunch service. The four years I'd worked for Seb, I had the routine down to a fine art. My parents were always complaining about me not making more of life but I loved my job and the people I met… some more than others evidently.

The groan that wanted to be heard was swallowed as I walked through the gorgeous dining room. The lighting cast dreamy shadows over the tables and the scent of expensive perfume and high-class food greeted me like an old friend. The comfort I got from being in the restaurant soothed some of the rough edges left by my sleepless night. I took my time checking everything was perfect before heading into the kitchen to collect a couple of glasses that I'd noticed were missing from one table.

With my mind on the task at hand, I didn't notice Seb until I nearly ran into him. "Sorry, I was a little distracted."

His face creased with concern. "Is everything okay, Scott?"

"Yeah, yeah. There are some missing glasses on table four is all." Seb's eyes narrowed but he nodded, saying no more. He didn't walk off though, like I'd hoped.

Was it that obvious something was up?

Then I recalled the dark rings under my eyes that I'd noticed when I shaved.

Saved from further conversation when Carl shouted for Seb, I left them to it. Returning with the glasses, I sorted table four. With one final check, I went to grab a quick drink, knowing it would be busy for the next three hours and I wouldn't get the chance to stop.

Well into my third hour of service, I felt a strange sensation at the base of my skull as I laid down the starters I held. The couple smiled as I asked if there was anything else I could get them. As they replied that they had everything they needed, I glanced about the restaurant, uncertain why I had an itch at the base of my skull.

My chest tightened and I was grateful I was no longer holding anything as my hands fell uselessly to my sides.

Oh dear god, what was he doing here?

Chapter 2

Luke

Exiting the taxi after Brett, I took a deep breath of the smoggy London air and willed the nerves in the pit of my stomach to behave. At this rate, I'd never be able to eat and Brett was already suspicious as to why I'd rung to see if he wanted to have lunch with me. The fact I'd managed to get a last-minute cancellation booking at La Trattoria Di Amore's chief restaurant left me thrilled and apprehensive at the same time.

Trepidation surfaced as my hands balled by my sides. I'd refused to acknowledge it this morning, but the lack of message that I'd been expecting from Scott was making me worry. I'd assumed after yesterday that he'd have been eager to send me a message as soon as he'd arrived at work. It was well into the afternoon service in the restaurant and he'd had hours to send a response to me. Why hadn't he messaged me? He'd been so eager that I wasn't sure what to make of it all.

Had he thought it over and decided I wasn't worth the effort?

Stop that right now!

It is not the time to start acting like a teenager mooning over some boy.

The internal discussion was interrupted as Brett nudged my arm. "Are you planning on going in or just standing on the curb all day?" His musical Irish accent was full of amusement as he stepped to the door and signalled for me to follow.

"No, I'm planning on waiting for the weather to change," I joked back.

He turned, his eyes crinkling as he threw me the V. "You promised me lunch and it's nearly two o'clock. My stomach is starting to think my throat has been cut, so get a shifty on."

"Dear lord, why do I bother with you," I grumbled as he opened the gleaming glass door.

"Because you love me," he declared in a dramatic tone that got the floor manager of the restaurant to glance in our direction.

I was convinced he'd been about to laugh, but the smile fell from his face when he caught sight of me behind Brett. A rather unpleasant sneer formed on his mouth and pulled me up short. Adam Grainger and I had unfortunately had several run-ins over the way I'd treated staff in the past.

It had been Scott that had borne the brunt of my short temper. The Daddy side of me had wanted him and instead of acknowledging it, I'd done my best to ignore it. I'd ended up reacting in a negative way that had done me no favours and placed me at the bottom of the nice guy category.

Had Scott said something to Adam about me?

With a warm flush of heat spreading up my neck, I stood taller and walked to the desk with a confidence I wasn't really feeling. "It's good to see you Adam. I have a reservation for two under the name Brett Louden." I wasn't sure why both men's brows rose, but it was Brett's comical expression as his emerald eyes widened that had my lips twitching.

Adam's gaze had narrowed on me, but he nodded. "Hello Mr Mason, it's a pleasure as always to see you. Please follow me, your table is ready." His tone was polite, yet there was an unexpected edge to it that suggested it was anything but a pleasure.

When he walked off, Brett leant into me and whispered, "What the fuck crawled up his arse?"

A chuckle got stuck in my throat as we followed Adam and Scott came into view. The sounds of muted conversation and soft music faded away as my heart leapt against my sternum.

His jet black hair gleamed like onyx under the soft lights. His pale face was turned away so I could look without interruption. The outfit he wore showed off his lean, trim body and my gaze was drawn to the black trousers cupping his pert backside. My hands tingled with the memory of how soft his skin had felt as I'd warmed it with spanks. Blindsided for a moment by the heady feelings that surged through me, I released a gusty exhale. Would he wear the lacy underwear to work?

Really? Thinking about that right now is what you want to do?

Trousers that a second ago were comfortable now felt more like a boa constrictor with my cock pulsing with arousal. With diners sat at eye level with my crotch, I shifted and closed my suit jacket.

My gaze continued to linger on Scott. Then his head turned towards me and our gazes met. There were so many emotions flickering over his face, I struggled to make sense of them before Brett diverted my attention.

"What the heck is up with you? You gonna sit down? I'm really starting to worry about your sanity today."

His exasperated tone got my feet moving while I avoided looking in Adam's direction as he pulled out the seat for Brett. With us seated, I cursed that my back was now to the main restaurant so I couldn't see where Scott was.

I eyed Brett and tried to come up with a valid reason for us to switch seats. Not finding one, I took the menu Adam offered. My brow furrowed at the hint of steel in his gaze.

What had Scott said to him?

The question nagged as Adam left us with the menu and a stiff smile.

I opened the menu and glanced at it, trying not to think about the reasons behind Adam's behaviour.

"I thought you said this was a friendly place?" Brett stated in a dramatic stage whisper.

Glancing across the table, I shrugged, unable to come up with an answer that didn't put me in a shitty light.

His gaze roamed the room behind me. "There is something decidedly off about the way he was talking to us. The words might have been pleasant but his tone could have cut you to ribbons like a knife."

Brett's ability to read people was second to none, although that was no big surprise with him being a doctor of psychology. We'd met a uni and, after a bit of a rocky start, we'd become friends. When Brett had suggested we rent a flat as the student digs were too noisy, I'd jumped at the chance. As neither of us were interested in the other, we'd stuck to friendship and it had lasted more than a decade. Because of that, we'd bunked together up until four years ago when Brett had gotten serious with his boyfriend. They'd wanted alone time, so I'd taken that as a sign and took the leap into the housing market.

I'd managed to buy a house in one of the suburbs of London, in an area that was going through regeneration at the time, so the cost hadn't been too astronomical. Not that I'd had to worry about that with my mother having given me some money from her grandparent's estate.

Pictures of my beautiful home came to mind, but with them came the feelings of loneliness the empty house often created.

The thoughts wanted to drag me down so I opted to tease Brett to distract myself. "Maybe he's not used to seeing someone as gorgeous as you and he's in shock." I grinned at him, though the thing was. I wasn't joking. Brett was stunning.

His golden hair was cut and styled back from his face. The layered cut was sophisticated and showcased his angular features. His emerald eyes looked as if they'd been polished and gleamed with humour most of the time, and his lips were full and dark pink. At five foot seven, he wasn't tall but his willowy frame made him appear taller, giving him a delicate air that belied the core of steel hidden beneath the surface.

Brett had known hardship in ways many would not be able to fathom and it was that understanding that allowed me to be honest with him about myself. He was also the only person I trusted enough to talk about Daddy kink and my father. He was also the reason I'd uploaded The App to my phone and reached out to SassyS.

"Oh shut up," he grumbled and then spoiled it by batting his long eyelashes at me.

"Good afternoon gentlemen, are you ready to order your drinks?"

Scott had materialised silently, causing my head to swing around and make me feel a little dizzy. My stomach dropped at his acidic tone and the face devoid of any emotion as he stared at Brett and totally ignored me.

An ache in my jaw alerted me to how hard I was grinding my teeth. Why was Scott not looking at me?

"Are we going to make an afternoon of it? If we are I'll have the rather delicious sounding porn star martini." Brett's lips made a smacking sound as he glanced from Scott to me, his shaped brow arching.

"I don't remember you saying you had the afternoon off? I have no plans, my calendar is pretty *empty* right now." I stressed the empty as I looked directly at Scott. It was hard to tell from his expression if he was getting my meaning at all.

"That's a change for you, it's normally chock-a-block rammed with appointments, meetings and god knows what else."

Brett answered me, but it was Scott that held my attention, specifically the look of confusion in his eyes as he glanced between Brett and me.

Fuck, what an arse!

Why had I thought that bringing another gay man with me to see Scott was a good idea? Did Scott think I was playing with him?

My thoughts were confirmed when Scott spoke. "Some people change from day to day, whereas others don't change at all, even when they say they want to." His voice warbled as sadness seemed to seep from him and suffocate me.

"Scott, I have changed, you have to believe me," I blurted out, feeling desperation take hold of my tongue.

With a look of disbelief, Scott froze and the panic inside me took hold. "Please, I never lied yesterday. I came here today because I wanted to see you and to find out why you haven't messaged me as you promised." I swallowed hard and took a step off into the abyss. "Do you want another spanking from Daddy for not doing what you said you would?" I growled, lowering my voice.

The choked cough coming from the other side of the table was ignored as I waited to see what Scott would do.

When his face pinked and he squirmed, my heart rate went crazy. I lowered my eyes to below his waistline and my body responded to what I was seeing. He clearly liked the idea, but would he be brave enough to follow my lead?

Chapter 3

Scott

I dragged my weary feet to the back door and gave a half-hearted shout of goodbye. The chilly night air washed over my exposed face as I stepped outside and thought about the trek to the tube station. So tired, I didn't initially notice the car sat at the curb as I exited the alley to turn down the road.

The sound of a shout had me glance at the car and my heart rate accelerated so quickly I lost the ability to inhale. As I gasped and struggled to keep it together, Luke got fully out of the car.

"Scott, would you like a lift home?"

It was hard to tell if it was concern I could hear in Luke's voice as his face was shadowed by the darkness. The conversation we'd had that afternoon came back to me and I halted.

"Do you want another spanking from Daddy for not doing what you said you would?"

I couldn't quite believe my ears though my cock, on the other hand, had no such problem. When Luke's gaze shifted to my crotch, my hands balled at my sides with the urge to conceal what was happening to me. Why would he go all Daddy on me in front of his... friend?

You heard what he said about the guy being gorgeous. *My gaze moved to the man sat opposite Luke and my arousal fled. For a moment, my heart had soared at Luke being so forthcoming about what had happened between us. Then the guy with Luke had made a choking sound and reality had come crashing back down on me. There was no way I could compete with this stunning guy.*

I glanced back at Luke, his face flickering with emotions that raced across his face so fast I couldn't read them, struggling to hold it together. Choosing to ignore what he'd just said, I asked in a flat tone, "Are you ready to order Sir or would you like a few minutes more?"

Luke's face looked crestfallen but he nodded at his companion. "Go ahead and order whatever drink you want, I'll just have some bottled water please."

The sound of footsteps coming towards me roused me from my thoughts as Luke stopped in front of me. The security light revealed the uncertainty written on his face.

Why was he here?

When he'd finished his meal he'd left without a word, his companion clinging to Luke's arm as they'd exited the restaurant. Not that I'd been paying much attention. *Liar, you couldn't keep your eyes off the pair of them.*

I stood still, waiting to see what Luke wanted and acknowledged the part of me that had hoped he wouldn't give up on me. As he stood dressed in casual trousers and a thick padded jacket, the wind caught his hair, and I wanted him to hold me, to tell me everything was going to be okay.

"Can I give you a lift home?" he asked again, hesitancy creeping into his voice.

"Why? You didn't seem all that interested today after you brought your *friend* to my place of work to throw him in my face." The petulant tone would have suited a five-year-old child, nevermind a grown man. But I couldn't seem to stop myself from trying to provoke Luke.

The air trapped in my chest refused to leave as Luke took a step closer, his body crowding mine as his eyes darkened. "Because we have unfinished business to talk about and I want to explain what a stupid prick I was for bringing my best *friend*, whom I've never had a relationship with, to meet you without explaining who he is."

The gusty exhale left me with hot cheeks as I tried to listen and reason with myself rather than jump on Luke. I wanted to demand he kiss me, to make me feel better and take away the hurt that had hung over me like a massive storm cloud all day. "He's only a friend?" I asked with hope.

"Yes, he is." Luke glanced at the alley behind me. "Listen, let's go sit in my car. It will be a damn sight warmer and we can talk in private."

I twisted to look behind me and saw Adam stood in the open doorway that I'd had just exited. I gave him a quick salute to let him know I was okay. I turned and pushed at Luke's arm. "Quick, before he comes over and gives me another lecture."

Luke's brows rose but he did as I asked. Once we were seated in the car, he didn't glance at me as he started the engine. "We need to talk and I don't want to do it while I'm driving, so we'll go to my place—"

"Erm… why your place? I've had a bloody long day and this will only make it longer." I moaned, not sure why the thought of going to Luke's home made me all kinds of anxious.

"It's not far from here and I'll take you home anytime you want. I just want a place where I know we won't be interrupted, please?"

It was the please that did me in and I relented. "Okay."

With that, he pulled away from the curb and I shut my eyes to stop me staring at him while I tried to figure out what his game was. Did he really want a relationship with me, or was he just messing with me?

Adam had been very vocal after Luke had left this afternoon. He'd argued, point-blankly refusing to believe that Luke was nothing but a nasty piece of work, that I was better off telling him to take a hike. And yeah, there was a little part of me that worried he was taking the piss, but then I'd recalled how he'd been with me and I couldn't make myself believe he was all bad.

Didn't we all have baggage that made us act differently? Not having much crap to deal with, other than that I couldn't find a man to be the Daddy I needed, I didn't want to be too judgemental about things I didn't understand.

Don't tell fibs, you have found a Daddy!

The insistent voice was pushed aside as the warm air coming from the heaters and the long day caught up with me.

My heavy-lidded eyes opened at the weight of a hand on my arm shaking me gently. "Scott, we're here." With no chance to respond, Luke was out of the car and had my door open. With my seatbelt unclipped, his muscular arms came around me, and I was lifted from the vehicle. Burying my face in his jacket, I inhaled his expensive cologne. My heart pitter patted with joy against my ribs. I felt safe, cared for and I couldn't make myself insist he stop and put me down.

Luke shifted back, his arms tightening around me as he moved to shut the car door. There was a flash of light and a clicking sound as he locked the vehicle before he started to walk. When he stopped, I raised my head and looked about. What I could see of the street spoke of money and affluence.

"I need to open the door, are you okay to stand?"

There was concern marring his features as I nodded. He lowered me to the floor and I clung on for a few seconds more before I reluctantly let him go. A little shaky from the tiredness and still groggy from the catnap, I waited for Luke to let us into his home.

The light illuminated the hall as he stepped inside and took off his coat. I hesitated until he encouraged me to come inside. As the door shut behind me, I took in my surroundings. Warmth surrounded me as I was captivated by the luxuriance of the place. The thick carpet was matched to the warm rose painted walls that housed no pictures. There was a small teak hall table that held keys and unopened letters. The air was scented with… thyme and something I couldn't quite pinpoint.

"Your home looks beautiful," I said without reserve, as I remembered how untidy my flat was with its second hand, scruffy furniture. Heat climbed up my neck with embarrassment at the very thought of Luke wanting to come into my home.

"Remind me never to invite you to my place." I chuckled with nerves.

"I'm sure your place is fine. And I'm not going to be reminding you of that when I want to get to know you properly." His tone brooked for no argument as he stood watching me with a masked expression. It was only his fingers constantly moving that said I wasn't the only one that was nervous.

"Would you like a drink? Something to eat?"

"A soft drink would be good, but nothing with caffeine in it or I'll be up all night and one sleepless night is enou…" I slapped the hand over my mouth when I realised what I'd said.

"A sleepless night? It must be contagious because I didn't sleep for shit last night," Luke offered up, his cheeks turning pink as he kept his gaze firmly fixed on me.

"I... it was... I..." Failing to find the words, I yanked at my hair in frustration and glanced at the carpet.

"It's alright Baby, come on. Let's go sit and I'll get you a drink." As he spoke he walked past the table and down the hallway towards a closed door.

I bit my lip as a sob caught in my throat at the use of the endearment 'baby'. Did he mean it?

Oh, stop it.

Relieved Luke couldn't see my face, I scowled at myself and followed him into what turned out to be a kitchen and dining space. The long room was divided into two parts. A long breakfast bar marked the kitchen side. The sleek grey kitchen and stainless steel appliances should have looked cold, but the muted green walls and autumnal coloured tiles he'd used gave the room a warm feel.

The other side of the room housed a teak table sat by a large window that had four dark brown leather seats around it. I squinted out into the darkness to see if I could catch a glimpse of the outside, then gave up when all I did was make my eyes ache.

"I've got orange, pineapple, and cranberry juice. Will one of those do?" Luke asked as he opened the fridge and poked his head inside.

"I'll take the pineapple please." I walked to the table, pulling out a chair I sat and nervously tapped at the table as Luke filled two glasses before coming to sit next to me.

I took a sip of the juice he sat in front of me, not sure I could now get a word out. My mouth dried up and my tongue decided to play silly beggars and stick to the roof of my mouth.

"Scott, look at me," Luke encouraged.

Raising my gaze from the table, I sighed in resignation. The need to please this man was going to be a real problem, mainly when he used what I was coming to think of as his Daddy voice.

"I want to set a few things straight and I want you to listen to me first. Can you do that?"

"Yes… Luke." My hesitation caused him to lean into me. Could he tell how much I wanted to call him Daddy?

His face relaxed and his hand crept across the table and stroked the back of mine. "There is nothing going on with Brett and me, and there never has been. As I said, he's my best friend from my uni days and we lived together as flatmates for years. He is the only friend who knows me and understands my… needs."

When he paused to take a drink, I gripped my glass, willing him to go on. "You said that The App was the first time you'd decided to… you know," I shrugged, my face heating as Luke tilted his head and one brow rose.

"Meet someone and try being a Daddy," he finished for me and I nodded.

"Brett was the one who told me about The App and encouraged me to explore that other side of myself. Though I'm coming to think it's not so much another side of me, but all of me," he finished, sounding none too pleased by the confession.

I, on the other hand, wanted to jump up and down with joy at what that could mean. *Hold your horses. You haven't sorted out anything... yet.*

"Are you saying you'd like to be a Daddy all the time in a relationship?" I warbled and clutched at my glass, my knuckles turning white as I worried I'd break the glass. *So much for hold your horses, you let those fuckers run right over you.*

My internal battle was halted as Luke answered.

"Yes, I think I am. I'm not sure what that means. But today, when you never texted me your shifts and then didn't answer me in the restaurant, I wanted to go all... Daddy on that sweet little arse of yours." There was a desire in the depth of his eyes as they darkened and they held me captive.

Licking my lips, I willed my thundering heart to behave as my ears buzzed. "I'm sorry... I was going to message you, but then Adam collared me. Things after that...well let's just say he went on and on about how horrible you'd been to me, and it made me stop and think. I didn't tell him anything about what we did." I rushed on when I could see anger starting to swirl in the depth of his eyes. "I couldn't help it. He knew I'd arranged a date. Fuck, he'd helped me pick you for Christ's sake." I groaned and released the glass to bury my head in my hands.

"Eyes on me boy," Luke demanded.

My head lifted immediately and I squirmed at the heated stare that was waiting for me. "It's okay, I spoke to Brett about you too—"

"I didn't tell him anything. I would never betray you like that... Daddy."

Chapter 4

Luke

My heart all but burst from my chest at hearing him call me daddy. I was off the chair before I could stop myself and dragged him up with me. My mouth claimed his in a brutal kiss. I lost all sense of time as I tasted his sweetness and lush lips as they opened for me. A groan rose and rumbled up my chest as his tongue glided against mine, his body pushing harder against me as if he couldn't quite get close enough.

Shivers raced down my spine at the feel of his gentle fingers stroking the hair at the base of my neck. All afternoon I'd berated myself for my own stupidity for taking Brett to meet Scott without explaining who he was to me. In the cold light of day, it had been a hard pill to swallow when Brett had pointed out how our flirty relationship could appear to others. That maybe I should have warned both Scott and him as to what I was doing. It had all seemed pretty reasonable when I'd thought surprising Scott with a visit at work would be something he'd like.

Thick bastard.

It was true, I'd given no thought to how it would look, or how I'd previously acted towards Scott in the restaurant. Why I thought everything would go swimmingly, I'd never know. *Yes you do, you let your other brain take charge.*

I worked to shut out the negative crap as I lifted my head and stared at Scott's dazed expression. His lips were puffy and glistened with moisture. The tug of arousal low in my belly wanted me to do more than kiss. With my chest heaving, I sighed and guided Scott back into his seat. His silver eyes begged me not to stop. My fingernails dug into my palms as I retreated from temptation.

"Stop it with the begging eyes," I pleaded as I took the seat I'd vacated. "We need to talk about this before anything more happens."

"But..." Scott hesitated, his eyelashes fluttering, "Daddy, I want more kisses." His mouth moved into an adorable pout as he stared at me with longing.

"Aw fuck... stop that right now," I demanded, holding up my hands as if to ward off his charms.

Like that will work!

His lips twitched and I sagged in the chair. "Daddy will have to punish you if you carry on with this nonsense," I threatened without any real heat, given that he clearly enjoyed having his arse spanked.

"I've been a very naughty boy Daddy… you should teach me a lesson," he whispered in a husky voice that did nothing to help me keep my resolve to talk first.

"If you keep this up, you are going to find out what happens to naughty boys in this house," I growled while I struggled to sit still, my cock painfully pushing against my trousers. The glow that lit up his face was enough to get me standing and walking to the counter to put some distance between us.

The mischievous expression faltered as he took in the distance between us.

"Listen Baby, I want a relationship with you. I don't want it just to be about fucking. I'm too long in the tooth for that. I… I want more. I want to see if we can put the past behind us and work on a meaningful relationship." As I spoke, Scott sat forward, his expression saying he was listening to everything I was saying.

When I finished, Scott's hand rose and pushed at the hair that had flopped over one eye. I held my breath as the silence lengthened.

"I'd like that but...what do you mean by relationship? Just boyfriends who date? Or do you mean being my Daddy... all the time..." he trailed off, his face hopeful.

God he slew me. No bloody wonder I'd struggled around him for all those years. The expression he wore did crazy things to my heart. I didn't want to think about all the emotions and feelings that were there, wanting me to acknowledge them. Had all these years of wanting him turned into something... more?

A ball of panic choked me for a second and pulled me back to the fact that I hadn't responded. As I inhaled, I met his yearning gaze with the sense my expression probably mimicked his and nodded. "Yes, I want it all... with you."

***

The next day I walked into the hotel feeling like I could take on the world. That was, until the receptionist, Lizzy, beckoned me over. Her tight blouse showed off her breasts to their best advantage as she pushed them towards me. I didn't flaunt that I was gay, but I'd made no secret of it either. Most of the staff had met my previous boyfriend Brody, so it always surprised me when the female members of the team flirted with me. As Lizzy fluttered her fake eyelashes at me, I worked at keeping the smile on my face.

"Good morning Lizzy, is there a problem?"

"Oh Mr Mason, I'm so glad you're here! There has been an incident with one of the guests." She lowered her voice, her eyes sweeping the reception before she continued in a hushed tone. "The wife of one of the guests found her husband in a compromising position with another woman. I'm sure you can imagine what they were doing." She giggled, her flushed face and bright eyes said she was clearly enjoying whatever she had conjured in her mind.

I, on the other hand, did not want to think about it.

"She got a little upset and attacked the woman. She was screaming and carrying on and the people in the next room reported it. But in the meantime, the woman that was attacked had called the police because the wife then started to hit the husband with one of our lamps," she finished on a breathless gasp.

"Where is everyone now?" I asked, seeing how my day was going to pan out. I heaved a sigh.

"The police, along with the security guard, Cooper, are trying to sort it out in the suite the husband had booked. The room is 1231."

As she finished, I noticed the other two receptionists stood off to the side, listening to Lizzy. I threw them a stern look as they tittered like school girls. "I'll drop off my briefcase and head to the suite. Please let Cooper know I'm on my way."

I stalked to the lift and tried to mask my irritation at having to deal with this nonsense. By the time I got back to my office three hours later, I was in no mood to have to face the hotel owner, who it seemed had decided to fly in special, just to have a meeting with me about the proposed changes to the lifts and the cost attached. I listened to Sarah as I glanced at my shut office door.

"Griffin has been waiting an hour and he's not in the best of moods right now."

"Did you explain where I was and what I was dealing with?" I ground out through clenched teeth. Pain throbbed behind my eyes as my body begged for some caffeine.

"I did, but you know what he's like," she whispered, her eyes never wavering from the door in front of us.

"It's all right. I'll go and deal with him as long as you get me some coffee." At her nod, I strolled into my office. My jaw bunched at the sight of Griffin Hudson slumped in my seat with his polished shoes sat on my desk, scrolling through the large tablet he held.

His jet black hair was kinked with curls and when he let it grow, it gave him a cherub-like appearance. The only thing was, he was anything but a cherub. He was a ruthless businessman who had worked hard to succeed in the hotel business. Rumour had it, he'd come from a poor family and he'd spent most of his youth in and out of borstals for all sorts of things. Then, at some point in his teenage years, he'd met a man who had changed his life and given him the opportunity to show that he wasn't just a thug.

His icy blue eyes never moved from the screen, so I strolled to the desk and sat down in the seat opposite him, praying Sarah would bring me my coffee before he'd finished whatever he was doing.

"You know, if you continue to grind your teeth like that, you'll end up needing veneers." His soft Scottish accent was barely noticeable as he spoke, his gaze shifting to me.

"Let's just say I've had a slightly fraught morning."

His lips tilted up at the edges with what appeared to be amusement, but it didn't touch the ice in his eyes. "Yes, I heard the police were here and that a man got caught dipping his wick in the wrong place."

I rolled my eyes. "If only. The stupid sod was sleeping with the wife's much younger sister. The two of them were going at it hammer and tongs. Even the bloody police didn't know quite what to do. There will be no sisterly love lost between them that's for sure."

Griffin's laughter filled the office as Sarah came in with my much-needed caffeine fix. Thanking her, I took the cup she offered.

"Do you need me for anything else?" she asked as her gaze moved to Griffin then back to me.

At his head shake, I responded, "No, that's all for now."

I sat back and took several sips of the coffee, letting the caffeine work its magic.

"So the figures you sent me for the lift alterations. There has to be a company that will do it for cheaper. Those bastards are trying to rob us blind. I've got my PA to list other companies that will quote for us."

The tension that had started to release returned as I sat forward and plonked my cup down. Coffee sloshed in the cup as I stood up and stalked to the window to look out, needing a moment to control the urge to argue. Griffin, when it came to money, was a hard-nosed bastard and I'd always struggled when he challenged me about the things I'd spent months working on.

"I've pissed you off again," he stated, with some amusement in his voice.

I swung around and tilted my head, eyeing him from across the room. He was a powerfully built man and though the suit was tailored to fit, and expensive, they never seemed to sit right on him. He somehow looked constrained and uncomfortable. "When is it any different? You hold every penny as a prisoner and then I have to spend hours explaining why we need to spend the money." I chuckled when he shrugged as if to say "and, your point is".

"We had an incident with one of the lifts just two days ago where it was stuck with people in it for hours." The interest on his face made me struggle to hold still with the memory of Scott still fresh in my mind. "We need that particular lift to be renovated before something happens and we get sued."

"Let's go take a look and we can talk about the figures for that lift first."

I released the breath I'd been holding, thankful he didn't ask who had been stuck.

As Griffin rose from my chair, a predatory smile lit his face. "Did you enjoy the time you spent in the lift?"

Fuck! Struggling to maintain my composure while I maintained eye contact, I gave him a stiff smile. “It was enlightening.”

I was sure he’d muttered “I bet” but I chose to let it drop as I opened the door and prayed he’d not ask any more questions.

Chapter 5

Scott

DaddyL: *Do you want to go out for something to eat tonight? I see you're only working till four o'clock.*

After reading the message, I shoved my phone back into my pocket, a beaming smile spreading across my face. Remembering where I was, I glanced about the staff room, checking no one was paying me any attention. With Theo, Sawyer, and Adam busy chatting, I sagged with relief against my seat.

Hell yes I wanted to go out on a date. I'd also like to shout about it from the rooftops, but with Adam watching me like a hawk all the bloody time, I'd need to wait to respond to Luke so as not to arouse suspicion.

I'd taken to keeping our dates a secret and doing my best to avoid any conversation where I'd have to tell a lie. I wasn't any good at telling fibs. My pale skin lit up like a fireworks display on bonfire night any time I tried. And anyone who knew me was aware of this, so staying quiet was the only solution.

The thing was, I really wanted to talk about Luke. I couldn't remember ever being this happy in a relationship before. Over the last few weeks, all my spare time was spent at Luke's house or we went out and explored London. We'd wrap up in warm clothes and trudge the streets, looking at the lights and the window displays. For me, they were magical moments, just being together.

What about when Luke takes you to his home?

I squirmed in my seat and tried my best to divert myself from the thoughts of Luke and how much he enjoyed embracing his Daddy side behind closed doors. Of how he'd bought me a special gift from my favourite lingerie shop.

"Scott, are you up for a few drinks after work? We're feeling the need to go out and cut loose a little bit," Theo asked as both Sawyer and Adam nodded at me eagerly.

Shit, how can I say no?

Think, come on.

With no immediate answer as to why I couldn't go, I reluctantly nodded. "I suppose so, but it can't be a late one for me. I have got a double shift tomorrow and I can't come in hungover again. Shit, Seb was not impressed when I knocked that glass of wine into that lady's lap the last time." I sighed dramatically.

"That was months ago and he forgave you as he was also a little worse for wear after that works night out," Adam pointed out, grinning at me.

The door opened and the man in question walked in. "Aren't you all supposed to be working here?" His dark brows rose.

There were several muttered "Yes" as we all got up and tidied up the cups and plates we'd been using.

"Scott, can I have a word with you please?"

Though it sounded like a request, there was no way I was going to say no to the boss. "Yeah, Seb."

When he turned to leave the room, Sawyer whispered in a childish voice full of glee, "You're in trouble."

"Oh fuck off," I responded, mimicking his voice.

He giggled and shoved me towards the door so I could follow Seb. "Go on naughty boy."

I bit my lip to stop the retort about how I was only naughty so Daddy could spank me and walked quickly after Seb, who'd disappeared. Heading through the noisy kitchen, the noise of which I no longer really noticed, I exhaled and tapped on Seb's open office door.

"Come in Scott, and shut the door."

My hands became clammy at the request. Doing as I was told, I stood by the now shut door. *What the heck was this all about?*

"You can take a seat, Scott," Seb gestured to the seat opposite him.

His face revealed very little as I took the chair and put my hands under my thighs, feeling them tremble. Was I in trouble? I tried to recall if I'd done anything that would warrant such a meeting that involved a closed-door to maintain privacy. Seb's door was only shut when he had important meetings and didn't wish to hear the clatter from the kitchen. The office, though a glass box, was soundproofed.

"What we talk about today, I'll ask that you keep the information to yourself."

As he started to talk, my heart skipped a beat and I pushed my thighs into my hands.

"You are aware that we will be opening a new restaurant?" Seb asked, his brow's pinched together.

I nodded and chewed my lip. There'd been some talk and gossip about it because nothing officially had been mentioned by either Carl or Seb. Adam had made reference to it, as had

Lenny, who was dating Carl's business partner, Nathan.

"I'd heard some talk about it." I wasn't sure if I should mention about it being above Nathan's BDSM club or that the Flamingo bar attached to the restaurant was going to be for people like him. Sawyer had been super excited to explain about what the club was all about. As Sawyer had been the one to trial The App that I'd had used to meet Luke, it made sense that Nathan would explain what he had planned. Sawyer had been only too happy to share his excitement with me. Not that I wasn't as excited as he was because I really wanted to be able to go out with my Daddy and act as we did in private.

Pulled from my wayward thoughts, I tuned back in to Seb, hoping I'd not missed anything vital.

"The restaurant is planned for an Easter opening and I'm starting to think about staff who might be interested in working in this new venture and possibly in the club as well. Nathan and I have talked about this extensively." His lips pursed and his face became thoughtful.

My stomach jittered as I sucked in a breath and tried to sit still.

"Richie advises me that he spoke to you about the... dynamics of our relationship." His brow arched as he kept his gaze on mine, as if searching for something. Richie had explained about Seb being a Daddy but as they were both private people, the details had been minimal.

"Erm… well… yes, he did… but he didn't go into any great detail or anything," I hurried to say. My face felt as if it was on fire by the time I'd finished.

"Thank you for clarifying that Scott," Seb said with some amusement. "I'm led to believe that you also have had a Daddy in the past?"

The bluntness left me at a loss for something to say for a second. It was surreal that I was actually talking about this with my stern boss, a man that didn't often show his softer side. Well, that was until he started to date Richie, I reminded myself.

I wasn't sure if it was because he caught me off guard or if it was my need to share that had me blurt out. "I have a new Daddy, Luke Mason."

His eyes widened and his face darkened. "You can't be serious?" he asked, sounding incredulous.

"What… why would you say it like that," I cried, tears blurring my vision at how harsh Seb sounded.

"Scott, that man has been nothing but awful towards you and… he… isn't a nice person." He glanced at his desk, a look of indecision on his face.

I was too upset to question what he meant, my chest hurt and the urge to cry increased. "You don't know him. Yes, he acted like a prick with me for a long time, but there were reasons for that. I swear, he's a great guy," I all but sobbed.

Seb's hands ran through his dark styled hair, ruffling it as his eyes hardened. "I'm not at liberty to discuss something that happened. But what I'm going to do is give you Ellie's number and I want you to ring him before you progress in your relationship with Luke, okay?"

My brow furrowed at the mention of his old office assistant. It had been nearly two years since Ellie had left. What the heck had this got to do with him?

"I can see from your expression that you aren't sure why I'd ask this, but please, do this for me. You'll understand once you've spoken to him. If you still wish to date Luke after you've spoken to Ellie then that's your choice because you'll have all the facts."

Panic gripped me by the throat at the tone he was using, suggesting that after the conversation with Ellie, I'd want nothing more to do with Luke. What the fuck was I missing here?

When Seb grabbed a pen and wrote on a piece of paper before sliding it towards me, I took it with trembling fingers.

"We've gotten a little off track. I brought you in here to offer you a position as head waiter in the new restaurant and bar. I'd still like to do that, if you're interested Scott?"

The smile didn't reach his eyes as he waited for me to answer. I wasn't sure what to say. I was still reeling from his request to ring Ellie. My hand tightened around the piece of paper I held. I clutched at it, giving it a glance before I stared at Seb. "I'd love the opportunity, but can I give it some thought first please?"

"Of course, there are still a couple of months before I'll need to move you to the site to help set up, if you're in agreement."

The excitement I wanted to feel at being given this opportunity was dulled by my worry. I don't remember what else was said once I'd left the office and headed back to work. The four hours seemed to drag until I could escape. The piece of paper felt like it was burning a hole in my trouser pocket.

With a sigh of relief I clocked out, only then remembering my agreement to go out for drinks, and that I'd not messaged Luke back. My hand shook as I pulled out my phone and saw there were three more messages from Luke, each a little terser than the last.

DaddyL: *Come on Baby, stop teasing Daddy. It's been five days since I've seen you.*

DaddyL: *There better be a good excuse as to why you aren't answering your Daddy?*

DaddyL: *I'll take this to mean that you aren't interested in a date night with me. I'll expect you to explain yourself to Daddy, sooner rather than later if you know what's good for you, boy.*

My heart sank at him thinking I wasn't interested in a date with him.

What had happened with Ellie?

Had Luke been in a relationship with Ellie?

My mouth pinched as I stared at my phone and then the empty locker room. Should I ring Ellie now and get it over with?

As I shifted to reach into my pocket for his number, Adam came barrelling through the door with Sawyer behind him. "You ready Scott? God I'm looking forward to relaxing and having a few cocktails. I've even managed to talk Richie into coming with us."

He carried on wittering, and I paid him no attention as I tried to figure out a good excuse not to go.

"Look at him, he's going to renege," Sawyer said, staring at my face.

A blush crept up my neck as I shook my head, "I'm not." I lied through my teeth, then silently cursed myself for not coming up with a reason. With thoughts of Adam, me and alcohol being a bad combination, I swallowed a sigh.

"Then come on, get your coat on. The bars are calling our names, and I for one am listening." He giggled and grabbed my arm, tugging me away from my open locker.

"Jesus, you just said get your coat and then you start dragging me out the door without it. You know it's winter right? And I'd freeze my arse off without it," I complained.

Adam swung back around, huffing loudly, and grabbed my coat before slamming my locker shut. He handed it to me with a put upon expression. "There you go, now get a wiggle on. Times a-wastin."

Chapter 6

Luke

Sitting on my sofa, I stared at my phone. What had gone wrong? Weeks we'd been seeing each other at every conceivable moment we could squeeze in between our jobs. It hadn't been easy to shift the meetings I'd had planned today to make sure I was free at four o'clock, after checking Scott's weekly schedule. Now all my effort seemed wasted and I was clueless as to why he hadn't responded to any of my messages.

We'd established a daily pattern where I'd message him when I got up and he'd respond, then he'd set about teasing me through the day with random messages and stories about what he might or might not be wearing under his clothes. Then when we were both home and in bed, if we had no plans, we'd face time so I could see him before he went to sleep. It was one of my favourite times of the day when I couldn't get to see him in person.

Our time off very rarely matched so I took what I could and if that made me a pitiful fool, then so be it. The screen on my phone lit up and for a second my heart jumped with joy. As I saw Brett's name flash up on my phone, I sighed and swiped to answer. "What?"

"Is that any way to greet your best friend?" he demanded, laughter in his voice.

"Yes it is," I growled back, staring forlornly out of the living room window at the dull, grey sky.

"Oh someone's in a grump. You want to talk about it, or do you want to go and drown your sorrows?"

There was something in his voice that had me say "Yes" even when that had not been what I was initially going to say. "Where do you want to meet?"

"There's a cocktail bar just down the street from my office at London Bridge, are you up for trekking into London?"

I didn't release the sigh, though it was a close call at the thought of getting a train and then a tube at rush hour. *You have fuck all else to do, now do you?*

With that ringing in my ears, I arranged to meet him at the bar.

I stood and glanced down at my causal trousers and jumper. With a shrug I went to grab my wallet and jacket.

Two hours later, I regretted my decision as I hardly managed to squeeze in through the throng of people crowding the bar, before spotting Brett at a table. It was thankfully tucked in a corner out of the way.

At the sight of two rather large empty glasses and the one full one containing a pink frothy liquid sat in front of him, I groaned. Something was wrong and as I searched his face, my heart sank. There was misery mixed with angry defiance and that was never a good mix.

As I slid into the seat next to him, I hailed the passing waiter. "Could I have one of those," I asked, pointing to Brett's glass.

The guy eyed it, smiled, and gave me a nod before walking off. Focusing my attention back on Brett, I braced. "What's wrong?"

His over bright eyes stared at me as one hand waved in the air, barely missing hitting me in the face. "I'll tell you what's wrong," he slurred, his eyelashes blinking rapidly. "He dumped me. The fucker! After five years, he decides he doesn't like my kinky arse and kicked me to the curb." He finished on a loud wail that caused several heads to turn in our direction.

I took hold of the hand that was determined to hit something and lay it on the table, covering it with mine. I took a second to think of something positive to say. Brett had given his all to please Nigel but it never seemed to be enough. For a long time, I'd wondered why Brett hadn't told the fucker to get lost, but I'd kept that thought to myself. Now, I wasn't sure how to broach the fact that Nigel was a spineless dick who over the last couple of years had shown his true colours.

"Things haven't been great between you two for a while. You had to have seen the writing on the wall when he went on holiday last month and you only found out about it from the note he left you on the kitchen table?" My teeth gritted together at the memory. It had to be soul-destroying to know your partner didn't have the balls to talk about shit.

Isn't that what Scott is doing to you?

The urge to punch something increased and I struggled not to crush Brett's hand.

"You'd think, with me being a doctor of psychology and all. But I thought he just needed some space. I didn't think he would use it to inhabit someone else's space with his dick!"

His voice warbled and he hiccupped before picking up his glass and taking a large gulp. For a moment I considered stopping him from drinking any more, then I took in the misery on his face and gave a resigned groan.

"Let's talk this shit out and then we can find a club so you can dance your pretty little arse off and find someone to remind you of what a catch you are—"

His face brightened when the waiter returned with not one but two drinks, stopping me from saying more.

"Thank you sweetie, but I don't remember ordering another drink," Brett said, beaming at the waiter, making the guy blush to the roots of his shaggy brown hair.

As I chuckled, I took the offered glass. "Did he order another before I got here?"

"No sir." The waiter twisted slightly and pointed back to the bar and a man sat on a stool. "The gentleman over there sent it."

Brett squinted and lifted the glass in a salute, offering up one of his deadly, sexy smiles. The waiter thankfully only had the empty tray, because I wasn't sure he'd have had the foresight not to drop it when his face and body went slack under the powerful sex appeal Brett was unleashing on the guy at the bar. The man seemed equally as enthralled as the waiter when I glanced in his direction.

I shook my head. “Dear God, stop now before you cause a riot. That fucking smile will get you into a heap of trouble.”

He glanced at me, the smile still firmly in place. “And your point would be?”

“Stop that right now you fucker, you know I’m immune to your charms,” I complained, but was happy to see he looked a little less miserable.

His mouth opened and whatever he was going to say next never came. Seeing something had caught his attention behind me, I swung around and froze in my seat. The lights illuminated the silky dark hair and milky skin I’d worshipped on more than one occasion.

What the fuck was he doing out with… Adam?

The paralysis lasted a few seconds longer as I watched Scott giggle and lean against Adam as he whispered into Scott’s ear.

Was this why he hadn’t messaged back? Had he made plans and didn’t want me to know about them? Did he not want to spend his free time with me anymore?

The questions kept coming, as did the anger that Scott would be so inconsiderate as to not to bother to message me back. He hadn’t spoken much about what his friends thought about our relationship. Was he embarrassed about me?

That question stung like a thousand bees, and I was up and moving before I could think to stop myself. Brett shouted after me, but I didn't stop to listen. My attention was focused on the man sat laughing with his friends. I stopped at the table and glanced at the four men sat around it. It took a moment for them to notice me and when they did, there were several different fleeting expressions on their faces, but it was Scott's that held me captive. There was regret and something I couldn't interpret.

"Good evening gentlemen, enjoying a night out are we?" Though I spoke to the whole table, my question was solely meant for Scott. He chewed his lower lip before lowering his gaze, saying absolutely nothing.

"We are, and if you don't mind, we'd like to continue it, so why don't you bog off," Adam sneered.

"Adam, stop! There is no need to be like that," Richie spoke up, his hand taking hold of Adam's arm.

Scott's flushed face lifted and his eyes gleamed with unshed tears. He looked utterly miserable as his mouth opened and shut twice before he muttered. "Please don't talk to my Daddy like that."

My heart stuttered in my chest, then took flight at the softly spoken words that stamped all over my doubt that this beautiful boy was mine.

The utter stillness around the table was instant. I was sure people would think we were playing a game of musical statues when no one moved or spoke for long seconds. Taking advantage of the shock, I walked around Adam and took hold of Scott's hand and pulled him from his seat, the reason I was actually in the bar completely forgotten in my need to get a few minutes alone with Scott and find out what had happened today.

Outside, the cold night air was bitter as Scott shivered in his thin shirt. I shrugged off my jacket and wrapped it around him. A smile lit up his face as he hugged the coat around his lean body.

"What happened today, Baby? Why were you not answering me?" I kept my voice down, praying I sounded calmer than I felt.

The smile dimmed a little and his lower lip wobbled as he glanced away then back at me. He stood a little taller. "Daddy, what happened between you and Ellie?"

Colour drained from my face and my knees buckled as I struggled to comprehend what he was asking. Who the fuck had told him about Ellie? Shit, shit, shit.

The curses on repeat, I struggled to come up with an honest answer that didn't make me look like a complete arsehole. "Remember when we talked about me being a horrible dick? Well, this was one of those times. I can't remember if I told you that Brody dumped me over the phone on Christmas day?"

He gave a small nod, his head tilting to the side as he brought his hand up and chewed on his thumbnail.

Sucking in the icy air, I thought carefully about my next words. "I didn't take it too well. I travelled to see him while he was on holiday and I made some threats when my ego took charge of my mouth. Weeks later, I found out that Brody had moved to the Isle of Man to be with his new boyfriend... I ... I..." I stuttered and exhaled at the look of expectation on his face. The lights from the bar seemed only to show off how pale he looked at my confession, and I hadn't even got to the worst part yet. I'd promised myself when he'd agreed to be my boyfriend that I'd be honest with him.

So I took another deep breath and rushed on. "I found a dead animal on the roadside and I boxed it. Unbeknownst to Ellie, I asked him to deliver it to Brody. It turned out Ellie forgot until the thing started to decompose in his home."

"Please stop! Christ almighty, tell me you're joking," Scott whispered, sounding utterly devastated, his fingers turning white as they clutched at my jacket.

His eyes begged me to take it back and I had to swallow my own tears to stop them choking me. "No Baby, I'm not going to lie." I took hold of his arms when it seemed like he was going to turn and run. "Please listen to me. I was stupid, hurt, and angry. I regretted it immediately. I was wrong and I've apologised to Brody and Nick, his partner. You have to believe me when I say I'd never do anything like that again. I swear on my life, I'd never do anything to hurt you," I begged, uncaring how I sounded as tears blurred my vision.

He stared at me, his eyes searching my face. "I need to think about this... think about us." With that, he wrenched his arms from my hands and ran off down the street.

For a moment I thought to go after him, but before I could get my feet to move, he disappeared into the crowded street.

Unsure how long I'd been stood in the freezing cold, I felt a warm hand touch my arm. Brett stood on the pavement, weaving slightly next to me. "He left then?"

Not at all sure how much he might have heard or seen, I nodded, the devastation not allowing me to do more.

"We're a right pair. Come on, let's go to mine. It will look better in the morning, isn't that what they say?" he slurred without conviction before he staggered to the edge of the pavement and hailed the first taxi he saw.

Scott will come back to me, he will. He has too.

Chapter 7

Scott

I barely resisted groaning as my back and arms strained to hold the big sofa my mother had insisted needed to be moved across the room to make space for all the people coming for the New Year's Eve celebrations.

"Scott for pity's sake, stop daydreaming and hold up the bloody end," Dad ground out as he puffed and panted while walking backwards, trying to avoid my Mum who was issuing instructions.

"I am holding it up as far as I can. The ruddy thing weighs a ton." I scowled at my Dad, not much better than him as I gasped for breath. My arms shook under the stress of trying to hold the sofa.

"Right there should do it," Mum said, giving us both a wide grin as we dropped it together and groaned in unison.

"I'm going to make sure I'm busy when she wants this thing moved back," I muttered under my breath to my dad, who shook his head.

"If I can't escape, then neither can you," he responded giving my shoulder a shove with his as he walked past, wiping his brow.

"I can be wily, don't forget," I shouted after him, making his shoulders shake with laughter.

He stopped at the entrance to the hall and glanced back at me with a grin that matched my own. "That's okay, so can I."

With that, he strolled out of sight. The feel of my Mum touching my arm had me shift to look at her. "Please don't tell me there's more to move," I begged.

"Oh shut up. You'd think I asked you to move the whole room around."

"You might as well have," I muttered back, only to receive a smack to my ear. "Hey, I could report you for child abuse, there are laws against smacking your child," I mock-threatened her.

"Well you show me the child and I'll make sure to keep my hands to myself," she responded, giving me another rap to my ear.

I rolled my eyes and went to sit down.

"Erm I don't think it's time to sit yet. We need to put out all the food for the guests." She tugged at my arm, not letting me go till we were in the kitchen.

"If I'd wanted to work I could have opted to do a shift at the restaurant tonight," I grumbled while filling the large trolley she'd bought years ago, and liked to use to shift the enormous amounts of food she always made when she had company. There was nothing more my mother loved than throwing a party. She always went all out on New Year's Eve, which was why I'd opted to work New Year's day in the restaurant, so I wouldn't disappoint her by not being here.

I didn't have any siblings so that meant I was expected to attend all family functions, not that I minded. We were a unit and nothing had changed that over the years, even when I'd come out. They were special people and I was aware of how lucky I was to have them.

When Luke had elaborated about how his father had been with him, I'd gained a new respect for my father. Although it had appeared on the surface that Luke's father had accepted him being gay, he hadn't really when he'd forced his beliefs onto Luke. The main one being he should only date high-powered men of a certain stature. With the need to please his father, it had forced Luke to hide his Daddy nature and his need for a boy to take care of.

The pity that always accompanied any thoughts of Luke's upbringing was quickly followed by confusion over his confession about the dead animal. It had been a couple of weeks since I'd seen him at the bar and he'd admitted what he'd done. It had taken me days to ring Ellie to find out exactly what had happened, when I wasn't wholly convinced that Luke had been honest with me.

He was, don't forget that!

My lips puffed out as I huffed and tried not to go down the rabbit hole of what was right and what was wrong with what he'd done to his ex.

"What's troubling you, Scott? That's the third time you've sighed or huffed and I know it's not got anything to do with helping me, so let me have it. What's going on?"

She eyed me with motherly concern and I put the plate I was holding down and went to her. Her arms opened immediately and she hugged me tightly. The scent of her favourite perfume, Miss Dior, wafted around me, comforting me with its familiarity. The love in her embrace had always set my world to rights, but right then I couldn't seem to find what I needed.

You need Luke!

Like that's gonna happen after you've not bothered to speak to him for weeks.

"Talk to me," Mum begged, sounding upset.

"I met someone... and... things are a little difficult right now." Not sure I wanted to discuss fully what had happened, I went with part disclosure. "He did something not very nice in his past and he told me about it and it upset me."

My mum eased back and lifted my chin to look at me. "Did he tell you willingly what he'd done?"

"Sort of, I'm not sure he would have mentioned it if I hadn't asked him."

"Did he hold anything back when you did ask?"

"No, he held nothing back from me," I answered with uncertainty. Where was she going with this?

"So, let me get this straight. He was honest with you when you asked outright and he didn't hide what he'd been like in the past. And this is a problem because?" Her lips pursed.

"I... we... I'm not sure." Why was it a problem? At the time all I'd heard was 'dead animal' and decomposing corpse, which Ellie had explained in graphic detail. It was that I'd got caught up on. Weeks, all I could think about was a dead animal in a box and why would anyone send that to someone they professed to love. It was just a little creepy and nasty.

It was in the past and he confessed to it without any pressure.

I scratched at my ear, unsure where that thought left me.

"Call him. Talk to him and see how he feels about family New Year's Eve parties," Mum encouraged as she let me go, giving me a gentle nudge towards the phone sat on the counter in the kitchen.

Was it as simple as that? Could I just ring him and see if he wanted to come to the party? He's probably already made plans with someone else. Maybe he has used The App to find another boy.

That thought turned my blood cold and my hand shook as it hovered over the phone.

"Go on, you've got nothing to lose," Mum said, before she left the room pushing the trolley of goodies.

Without giving myself time to be talked out of it, I grabbed the phone and took the chicken's way out, opening The App.

SassyS: Hey, are you busy tonight? I've got a New Year's Eve party to go to and I wondered if you wanted to come with me??? 😊

That is so lame.

That was enough to make me hesitate as I read it twice then quickly hit send. The moment the message delivered I started to hyperventilate. What if he doesn't answer? What if he does?

Bollocks, stop this crap.

With that running through my mind, I put the phone down and picked up a couple of trays of food. I'd not taken more than three steps when my phone buzzed. I swung back around so fast the tray tipped and pastries toppled to the floor in a creamy mess. "Fucking hell," I screeched and dropped the dishes back on the side. As I glanced at the door, I prayed I could salvage some of the food. My mother was going to go nuts if she came back and found this mess.

Crouching down, I scooped the smashed ones into a pile, then went to retrieve some kitchen roll to pick the others up to throw away. I'd managed to get most of them off the floor before I heard the sound of someone walking down the hall.

Shitttttttt.

I swiped at the creamy mess, smearing the lino and making it even more apparent that I'd had an accident.

"What did you do?" Mum enquired, with more calm than I expected, as she entered the kitchen and her gaze landed on the half empty tray on the side.

"Sorry." What more could I say as she shook her head and walked to the counter, avoiding the mess I'd created.

"You know, sometimes I wonder how you ended up as a waiter when you can be so clumsy." She sighed, sounding exasperated.

"Hey, I'll have you know I got a promotion. I'm now head waiter of the new restaurant and bar Carl and Seb are investing in—"

"When did this happen? Why am I only finding out about this now when you've been here for hours?" She glared at me, making me hunch over.

Why didn't I message her about this? Too bloody late now, you're going to have to face the music.

The sound of my phone buzzing again reminded me of what I'd been doing before the cake disaster. I ignored my Mum as I moved to snatch up my phone.

Convinced my heart was going to leap right out of my chest, I had to lean against the counter before I could make myself look to see who the message was from. With trembling fingers I swiped at the screen and let out the breath I'd been holding.

DaddyL: *Oh baby, I'd love to come. Can you send me the address?*

DaddyL: *Do you need me to come and pick you up, I should have asked first.*

There were several eye-rolling emoji's at the end of the second message and a stupid grin lit my face.

"I take it that is from your man?" Mum enquired as she strolled closer to look down at the screen.

"Tut tut. I can assure you, you don't want to be looking at that." I moved my hand and tried to keep a straight face as she eyed my hand and then looked at my face.

"Are you into something kinky?" she asked, her cheeks turning rosy as she continued to glance between my hand and face. There was curiosity, if I wasn't mistaken, but nothing else, so I answered as truthfully as I could without scaring her.

"Yes I am, but it's nothing heavy duty and you really don't need to know more than that," I finished, holding up my empty hand to stop the questions I could see coming my way.

"You're no fun," she joked.

I was relieved when she changed the subject, because who really wanted to talk about their kinks with their own mother. Not me, that's for sure.

"You'd better answer your man and then you can get the mop out to clean the floor, while

I try to figure out how to hide the gap on that tray." Her gaze went to the half empty tray, then her brows rose and I froze.

"Did you put back some of the pastries you dropped on the floor," she demanded, her hands going to her hips as she turned her steely gaze on me.

"Well... you see... there were... some that—"

"Stop right there!" The rosy bloom on her cheeks darkened and I struggled to stand still.

"I'm sorry. I'll make another batch if you want me too." I batted my eyelashes, offering her a hangdog expression.

"Oh please, you can stop your messing, I haven't fallen for that expression in years." She spoke with very little conviction and I had to bite my lip to stop smiling.

"Mop the bloody floor and I'll salvage this mess, but if you drop any more food I'll be pulling out baby pictures of you to show your man when he gets here."

With that threat, which I knew damn well was real, I rushed to clean up the smeared creamy muck off the floor. Only when I'd finished did I send Luke a message with directions and explaining he didn't need to collect me.

There was no set time for the party to start and I'd told Luke this. Two hours later, I realised my mistake when there was no sign of him and my anxiety levels had reached an all-time high. So much so, I'd been banned from helping and was now on coat duty. As the house started to fill with aunts, uncles, cousins, and friends, I began to wonder if I'd made a mistake inviting Luke to such a public event with the whole of my family.

We'd not even mentioned introducing each other to our parents. Now I was going to have him come and meet my whole family. *Like this is not going to scare him off.*

"Scott, how are you gorgeous boy? It seems like forever since I've seen you," Aunt Tina asked as she handed me her coat and then gave me a hug. Her face was flushed from the cold and her eyes twinkled with merriment. I loved her dearly because she was the black sheep of the family, always off on some adventure.

She was my father's sister, standing at six foot in her stockinged feet she tended to tower over everyone in the family. Even more so when she wore her beloved high heels, of which she must have had hundreds of pairs of.

"It has been six months, I think. You were off to somewhere in Africa."

"Oh gosh, it really has been forever." She took hold of my arm, drawing me with her into the lounge. "Come on, fill me in on all the gossip. Have you managed to bag yourself another boyfriend yet?" Her shapely blonde brows rose and her gaze turned serious. She hadn't liked my last boyfriend. In fact the feeling had been mutual. The minute they'd met they'd hated each other. I'd never figured out whether it was because they were both so similar, domineering and had a tendency to take over.

I never got a chance to answer her as I felt an itch at the base of my neck. I swung around and became immobilised when I met a pair of familiar hazel eyes.

Chapter 8

Luke

I'd been on tenterhooks the whole taxi ride over to what it now transpired was Scott's family home. When the woman opened the door to me, it had been Scott's eyes peering out at me from her face that had alerted me to where I was. Her youthful face showed how much her son had inherited not only her eyes but the smile that was lighting her face.

"Hello, can I help you?"

"Erm… yes, Scott invited me," I stuttered and did my best to keep control of my embarrassment at finding myself face to face with Scott's mother.

"Oh you must be Luke. It's so nice to meet you. Come in, come in, it's freezing out there." She carried on talking, not stopping to take a breath. A small hand took hold of my arm and guided me through the doorway. Only she never let go after she'd slammed the door shut. She kept hold and encouraged me towards a room that appeared to be overflowing with people.

I wasn't sure what I'd expected when Scott had messaged me. The mention of a party gave me images of a small gathering, not this full-on house party. As I glanced about, there must have been well over sixty people crammed into the room and I could hear voices coming from other rooms too. Any idea I'd had of getting a few minutes alone with Scott died as I found him with a beautiful, tall, statuesque woman who was grinning at him with a mischievous smile.

I was sure I was rude as I stood transfixed, taking in the man that I'd continuously been thinking about. I couldn't find it in me to care what his mother thought as my gaze swept over my beautiful man. The feelings of desperation I'd been living with for the past two weeks, feelings that I'd never see him again, wouldn't release their hold over me. The part of me that thought I'd lost my chance with him refused to let me look away from him in case he disappeared.

His hair shone liquid black under the lights. His pale face had splashes of colour riding over his sharp cheekbones. His dark fitted jeans and black shirt made my mouth turn dry. There was something so alluring about him that called to me on every level.

Unsure what had alerted him to my presence, his gaze shifted from the woman he was talking with and met mine. I gulped and my hands twitched at my sides with the need to touch him. To feel his soft skin. To know that he was real and that I wasn't going to wake up and find myself in bed, having dreamed this whole thing up since he'd messaged me.

Time seemed to stand still as he started to walk towards me, a smile spreading across his face as he reached me. It was only then that I noticed the fur coat he held in his arms.

"Are you trying out a new style, Baby?" I quipped, hoping to break the sudden tension that seemed to form when Scott glanced from me to his mother, who I'd completely forgotten was stood next to me.

"It's Auntie Tina's, I'm on coat duty..." he trailed off looking none too happy with himself as his feet shuffled and his gaze became fixed on the floor.

"Dear God, what is it with the youth of today." The disgruntled sounding comment from his mother made my lips twitch.

It took a concerted effort not to laugh as I pointed out, "I'm probably not that much younger than you, but I'll take that as a compliment."

"Shoot me now," Scott muttered under his breath at my comment and I struggled to contain my humour.

When all his mother did was shrug, Scott lifted his head. "Mum, behave. You'll frighten him off before he's even taken his coat off," Scott stated, doing his best to avoid looking at me.

That will not do.

"Scott, do you want to show me where to hang my coat up?" Although I'd phrased it as a question, I waited till he met my gaze to show it wasn't.

His face looked resigned as he walked around me towards the hallway. Once there, he checked to see if I was behind him. "I've been storing the coats in my old bedroom." Without any further explanation, he strolled up the stairs.

My stomach fluttered at the thought of being alone with him, and I hurriedly walked after him. Any idea about talking flew right out the window the minute he shut his bedroom door and threw the coat he held on the bed. I wasn't sure who moved first, him or me. The next thing I knew, my arms were full and I was kissing him hard on the mouth. Desperate moans and whimpers were the only sounds in the room, and I wasn't quite sure who was making them.

His hot mouth opened under my insistent lips and my tongue swept into his mouth. God I'd missed the taste of his sweet mouth and the feel of his body against mine. I couldn't seem to get close enough as I shifted and wrapped my hands under his bottom, encouraging him to wrap his legs around my hips as I lifted him up.

The moment his groin met mine, my legs buckled. I blindly moved until I felt the edge of the narrow single bed I'd noticed when I entered the room. I twisted and managed to sit without dropping him, not once releasing his mouth. My chest heaved as he clung to me, his mouth urgent and needy.

"Daddy, I'm so sorry," he muttered in between hot, wet kisses. "Please forgive me."

As the words registered past my haze of lust, I lifted my head. Breathless and a little giddy from the passion I could see swirling in the depths of Scott's eyes, I struggled to get my mind to remember why I'd stopped in the first place.

Forgiveness, yeah that was it.

"Baby, it's me that should be sorry. If I'd told you about what had happened in the past then you wouldn't have been blindsided like that. We could have talked about it. Worked it out," I finished, not entirely convinced I was making the situation any better.

His hands came up and took hold of my cheeks, his thumbs gently caressing the stubble on my face. He gave me an earnest look. "I… I'm not sure that would have made any difference."

My heart stuttered.

"But you're right, I was blindsided and it was a little shocking to think that you were capable of being…"

"Nasty. A prick. A stupid shit," I added when he stopped.

He chuckled, his eyes alight with amusement. "You know, if I'd have said those things, you might have felt inclined to spank my bottom for being cheeky." His mouth inched closer to mine, his hot breath mingled with mine. "Maybe I should spank Daddy for being naughty and teach him what happens in this *house*," he rasped in a sexy tone that did nothing to help me keep control of the desire bubbling inside me.

"Oh you're asking for trouble aren't you? You know fine well we can't do anything in your parents' home." I growled for effect.

His body rippled on my lap. "Daddyyyyy… you did that on purpose," he whined, his backside grinding down on my erection as his own pushed against my stomach.

My hands cupped his arse. My fingers roamed over the fabric and my brows rose. "What are you wearing under these trousers?"

His eyes got a delicious glint in them as he wiggled his bottom against my hands. "A little new year surprise for you," he whispered, his eyelashes fluttering at me.

"Oh fuck, you're trying to kill me aren't you? We haven't resolved anything and you're already determined to drive me nuts," I complained, even when I could hear the adoration in my own voice.

"Of course, it's what a good boy does for his Daddy." His earnest expression was ruined by the mischievous smile that followed.

"I've had nothing but you on my mind for weeks, and I don't want to start this New Year with unresolved problems. So we will talk first, my sweet Baby." The lack of confidence in my tone was pitiful.

He pouted at me and sat back and crossed his arms over his chest. "Go on then, but you're on a tight deadline Daddy," he said in a sulky tone that did nothing for my resolve to talk about what had happened in my past.

His chin poked out at me and I took a couple of breaths to steady my racing pulse. "We've talked a little about my father, but I suppose until recently I hadn't realised how much his opinion had been guiding the way I lived my life." When his face showed confusion, I tried to find a better way to explain myself. "I don't just mean the men I dated, but the way I behaved as well. The only time I was ever myself was with Brett. We had quite the heart to heart after we'd seen you. He wasn't aware of all of my... crappy behaviours, shall we say. Anyway, after our chat he pointed out that I couldn't live my life that way, trying to be two different people to please a parent. A parent who died some years ago and whose expectations I was still trying to live up to. It seems that Brett thinks I've not been living my life, but more existing in it."

Scott's gaze turned thoughtful but he didn't interrupt me.

"Not that I hadn't figured that bit out for myself! The thing was, I'd got so used to hiding behind the dickish behaviour that it felt normal. What Brett pointed out was, with the right people, I can be a different person. With him I've always felt comfortable and I feel the same with you." I sucked in a breath. "I want to stop hiding and be the man I'm meant to be, not the version my father wants me to be."

His teeth appeared as he chewed on his lower lip, his gaze intent on me. "Oh Daddy, I know you've never hidden from me. I've given a lot of thought to us over the last couple of weeks." His eyelashes lowered but not before I saw the hurt in his eyes. "I'm not bothered anymore about the way you were, because I know how you are with me in private." He swallowed and his arms opened as he leant in and hugged me to him, his face going to the crook of my shoulder. "I was upset for two reasons. One, that it's a lot to take in that the man you like, *a lot,* could be capable of being nasty, and two, that I was listening to other people's opinion and letting them cloud my judgement."

Where his skin touched my neck, it heated as he buried his face when he finished talking. His slim body shook and the sounds of sobs rose up.

"Oh Baby. It's okay. Come on, don't cry." My voice broke as he sobbed harder, pressing his wet cheek against me. "Daddy's got you. We'll work this out together."

His face lifted but where I expected to see at least a smidgen of relief, all I got was misery. "I… was… hiding our relationship, Daddy," he confessed, his face filled with pain.

That confession was like a punch to the gut, but I kept my expression neutral. "Do I look cross?" I asked, cupping his cheeks gently and encouraging him to look at me.

"No." I could hardly hear his whispered reply as his wet eyelashes dipped, shielding his eyes.

"That's right, Daddy is not mad. I get it, my sweet Baby. I'll also understand if you want to keep this relationship secret for as long as you need to, till you feel comfortable, okay?" I kept my tone light, even as my jaw ached.

This wasn't about me. This was now about my man's needs, so I gave him a genuine smile and prayed that we could work through this, together. If the idea of not being able to be open with him in front of the people he knew made my stomach clench, then he didn't need to know that. I'd wait for eternity if need be, because these last two weeks I'd learnt something I'd already suspected since I'd claimed him as mine in the lift all those weeks ago. I loved him. I'd do anything for him, no matter what it was. He held my fragile heart in his hands, whether he knew it or not.

"Daddy… I don't want to hide you. I want everyone to know that you're… mine."

There was a hesitation and a lack of conviction that I chose to ignore. "Yes yours, as you are mine sweet Baby," I choked past the ball of emotion lodged in my throat that made my eyes burn.

He pressed his face back into my neck once more and inhaled. "That's good, because you'll have to explain to my parents why we've been up here for so long."

Laughter rose up as he giggled and sucked on my neck for a moment, before lifting his head to give me a shy smile. "You want to meet my family?"

Chapter 9

Scott

With Luke's agreement to meet my family, we'd reluctantly returned to the party, after paying a visit to the bathroom to splash some cold water on my face. I did my best to keep away from my mother and what I knew would be a twenty question interrogation.

With Luke touching me or laying his hand on my lower back, I'd had to stifle several moans. It finally sunk in after the second hour that he'd figured out what I had on. His fingers were frequently sneaking beneath the band of my jeans to play with the pearl beads that were part of the thong I wore. A thong he'd bought for me that I'd not had the opportunity to wear, until tonight. Now I was convinced he was making it his mission to torment me.

Who knew that the tiny little pearls rubbing against my flesh would cause me so many problems? Twice I'd had to excuse myself from a conversation to go to the bathroom and try to calm down.

Luke, the fucker, was well aware of what he was doing, trying to turn the tables on me. His fascination with what I wore under my clothes started early on, and it was something he'd started to ask about daily. It was something I'd missed over the last couple of weeks, the teasing banter and sneaky pics I'd take to send to him when he was in meetings.

"What's put that expression on your face?" Luke asked in a hushed voice next to my ear.

Uncertain what my face had revealed, I wrapped my arm around his waist and lay my head on his shoulder. "I was thinking about how much I missed you these last couple of weeks," I answered honestly.

My mother, who'd been talking to Aunt Tina, gave us both a sappy smile that caused me to roll my eyes at her. I lifted my head back up, not needing any more of her cooing over us. As I huffed, my dad started to shout, "Ten. Nine. Eight."

I shifted so I could face Luke and lifted my gaze to stare into his dark hazel eyes. My heart leapt at the expression he wore.

Was that love I could see?

It sure as hell looked like it. My mind blanked as my dad shouted Happy New Year and my lips were crushed against Luke's in a hungry kiss that rocked me to my very foundation. There was so much emotion in it, I couldn't catch my breath. My heart swelled and I longed for it to be real, that this New Year I'd find the happiness I'd been searching for. The thought was lost under a deluge of pure desire as large, warm hands held me tight and made the world disappear.

The rest of the night went by in a blur of kisses and hugs before Luke was able to get us out of the house and into the waiting taxi he'd had the foresight to book before coming to the party. As I slid across the seat, I heard my mother shout her last goodbye as Luke climbed into the cab behind me.

Luke rattled off the address before his large body pressed me back into the seat and he claimed my mouth for a brief moment. "You're all mine now," he rasped, before his mouth took mine in a blistering kiss.

Aware that we didn't have any privacy with only the glass partition between the driver and us, I tugged on Luke's hair. "Daddy, you've gotta stop, the guy can see us," I gasped as his mouth moved down my neck and he bit at the junction of my shoulder.

"I know, but you've been teasing me for hours." His answer was lost in my neck as it was assaulted with his lips and tongue. The roughness of his stubble abraded my sensitive skin and a shudder rippled through my body. My cock rubbed against the silky material of my underwear as the pearls rubbed against my pucker.

I clenched my thighs together in the hope of stopping some of the torment, then Luke's hand moved and lay against my hard length and I was lost. My head flopped back against the seat and I panted and gasped as he shifted some of his weight onto my body.

"Erm matey, I don't mind a show as much as the next man, but come on. You gotta stop before you forget you're in a taxi," the driver ground out. He sounded more than a little disconcerted by what he was witnessing in his rearview mirror.

I stifled a chuckle as Luke complained under his breath and got off me. He shifted as far away from me as the seat would allow.

With a devil prodding at me, well that and several glasses of champagne, I spread my legs. Only when I saw Luke's gaze shift back to me in the dimly lit cab did I start to stroke my cock over my jeans.

There was a groan and a stifled curse but he didn't move any closer, despite his eyes never straying from my hand. With a quick glance at the driver to make sure he wasn't paying attention, I slid down my zip. The lights outside the cab caught the pink satiny fabric of my underwear as I worked to free my cock. The tip popped past the band and looked obscene pressed against my abdomen by the innocent-looking silk. I lifted my hand to my mouth and sucked on a finger until it was dripping wet, then moved the wet digit back to my leaking cock, slowly circling the head. I bit my lip to stop the groan escaping at feeling the slippery glide of my finger over the sensitive slit.

My gaze was riveted to Luke as his chest heaved, his heavy-lidded gaze fixed on my fingers as I teased us both. My thighs shook as the pleasure urged me to do more than tease.

"No. You want to tease Daddy, then you can carry on what you're doing. You're not allowed to do anything to make yourself come." The strangled whisper stopped my hand from going to grip my hard length.

My jaw ached as my lips clamped together on the protest. I was so close to coming, my balls were heavy and my cock wouldn't require much more stimulation. But I did as I was told and teased the slit, spreading pre-cum all over the head. My eyelids drifted shut as images of Luke's mouth around my cock filled my mind.

"We're here," came the disgruntled voice from the front of the cab as I was jerked from my imagination.

With heat spreading up my neck and cheeks, I was grateful for the dimness in the back of the cab. My clumsy fingers tried to shove my cock back into my jeans as Luke paid the driver.

Chuckles came from Luke, but I refused to make eye contact with him and instead I got out of the cab. The icy evening air took my breath away and cooled my ardour as I waited for Luke to join me.

I refused to insist he hurry as he took his time getting out of the car and then took my cold hand and walked at a snail's pace to his front door. If he was trying to pay me back, it sure as hell was working.

When the door was locked behind us and he turned to face me, I exhaled embarrassingly loud at the stark need in his hazel eyes. I didn't get a chance to do more than open my arms before I was lifted up and carried up the stairs. The show of strength renewed my flagging arousal and I ground against him, my mouth trailing kisses up his neck to his ear. He growled as my teeth sank into the fleshy part of his earlobe.

"Daddy… Daddy you need to hurry up," I moaned as he stopped at the top of the stairs.

"You're a very naughty boy. Do you think you have the right to tell me to hurry up after what you did in the cab?" His gaze met mine and I nearly swallowed my tongue at the gleam in his eyes.

Slowly lowered to the ground, Luke made sure to rub every part of me against him before he released me. "I think Daddy needs to teach you a lesson. Take off your clothes here, with the exception of the pretty little thong," he rasped, his voice sounding as if it had been scraped with sandpaper.

I glanced about the hallway, my brows rose but when I took in his fierce expression I started to strip out of my clothes without a word.

The front of my silk thong was dark, evidence of how aroused I was. His eyes darkened as he stared at me. I stood tall, knowing that regardless of the fact I was on the skinny side, Luke found my pale body attractive. He'd spent hours tracing the tattoos around my thighs with his lips. His fascination with them never failed to amuse me, especially when he'd stated he wasn't into tattoos of any kind usually.

As he stepped towards me, then sidestepped me to go into the bedroom, my brows pinched together. *Where was he going?*

As if he'd heard my silent question, he answered me. "I bought you a Christmas present and I think now is the perfect time to give it to you." There was an unmistakable edge of amusement to his voice that caused my stomach to dance in anticipation.

He disappeared into the spare bedroom next to his, so I stood and waited to see what he'd bought me.

As he returned, my heart rattled against my ribs and my breath got stuck somewhere between my chest and my throat, my eyes widening.

"I noticed you have a tendency to ask for me to smack you harder, which got me to thinking. Maybe a paddle would give you what you want."

As he spoke, the red leather paddle was held up for my inspection. One side was more padded than the other and my arse clenched at how it would feel with each spank Luke gave me.

He walked back to the stairs and my hands balled at my sides. My cock leaked against the already sodden silk. He stepped down several steps before he turned to face me and beckoned me closer. "I want you to kneel on the stairs and face the top."

Hyperventilating at the speed at which I moved to do as he bid, I knelt on the second step and rested my arms on the top step, bracing for what was coming. My whole body vibrated with the thought of what was about to happen. I'd never had anyone use a paddle on me before and I was thrilled that Luke would think about my needs in this way.

I'd never have had the courage to ask him to buy something so he could smack my bottom the way I'd dreamed of. It was a little unnerving that he'd picked up on my need when none of my other Daddies had.

That thought flew right out of my head as my body jerked at the first spank to my backside. I jerked forward at the force and the painful sensation took my breath away, but I knew it would turn to pleasure soon enough. So I pushed back, even as my eyes watered and my bottom cried for me to move away from what was coming. The hum that came from Luke as I held my bottom higher caused my heart to soar.

The sound of the paddle cutting the air was the only warning I got as I was spanked again and again. Heat morphed and spread through my lower body. My cock pulsed and leaked against the satin. The friction was maddening as I rocked into the spanking, needing more.

With sweat slicking my skin, my hair stuck to my face as my vision blurred and I cursed and cried out, oblivious to what I was saying with the sensations bombarding me. As my chest heaved and my mouth dried, my whole body felt on fire and suddenly I couldn't seem to find my bearings. The entire world seemed to shrink down to the feelings flowing through me.

"Daddyyyyy... oh Goddddd... helpppp meee," I screeched as my back bowed. My cock pulsed and bucked, cum soaking through my underwear as I mewled, held in the grips of my pleasure. The world faded to white as my body was held for long seconds in the throes of my orgasm, blinding me to everything.

As I collapsed in an exhausted heap against the carpeted stair, wet heat hit my backside and I shuddered. Wetness spread over my hot arse and I grinned as Luke's cum slid down my body in ownership.

Chapter 10

LUKE

"Luke, are you free to talk to Griffin? This is the third time he's called and he sounds even more pissed off than the last time." Sarah's voice came through the intercom, interrupting my thoughts.

Seeing as my last meeting had finished ten minutes ago, I saw no way out. Griffin would continue to ring every half hour until I responded, and with Sarah already sounding frustrated I answered, "Yes, I am. Put him through."

I was convinced she hadn't even heard the last part as Griffin's voice came through the speaker a nanosecond later. "Why the fuck are you avoiding me? I've left three messages for you to ring me back," he blustered, sounding irritated.

"Hello Griffin, nice to hear from you. I have had back to back meetings all morning. I do have a hotel to run." The edge of sarcasm was totally lost on Griffin as he barrelled on.

"That might be the case, but I have fifteen hotels *I need* to oversee, so quit ignoring me. Have you gone through the list of builders that May sent you? I was expecting those quotes on my desk by now."

I didn't point out the fact he didn't have a desk because he refused to be tied down to one place. All paperwork was sent to his PA, May, who was based at the head offices on the other side of London.

The one and only time I'd been for a meeting, I'd found that May, a stern-looking woman in her fifties who would have made a great dragon, had the office which should have been Griffin's. I'd not had the courage to ask him about it, so when he'd left I'd asked May. Her only response was a stiff-lipped, stern expression that said mind your own business.

I swallowed a sigh. "You do know that it's only been two weeks since New Year and that everyone is busy trying to catch up from the holiday season—"

"Whatever bullshit excuse you're about to give me, stop. I want those quotes by the end of next week. I need to decide if we should go ahead and start on *your* favourite lift with the builder you've picked or use another firm with a better quote."

This time the sigh did escape. It would seem that Bob had been all too aware of what I'd got up to in the lift to distract Scott and had gossiped about it. That information had found its way to Griffin, who seemed to think it was highly amusing to keep referring to it.

I'd got over my embarrassment weeks ago, but that didn't mean it didn't still piss me off when he made reference to *my* lift. Thankfully, the years of working for him allowed me the privilege of being frank with him. "You know you seem to have an unnatural fascination with me and what happened in that lift. You know that right? This has to be the tenth time you've mentioned it." I chuckled at the string of curses coming down the speaker.

"Get me the bloody quotes." With that, the speaker went silent and the grin I'd developed dropped a little at how much work he'd possibly added to my ever-growing list. Having to meet a dozen new builders and go through the hotel did not fill me with joy, especially as I'd planned to take a few days off to spend with Scott.

There had been an incident on New Year's Eve involving one of Scott's work colleagues and Scott had been more than a little upset by it. He hadn't gone into detail, but I'd seen the news and figured out what had happened at Nathan's club, The Playroom.

The police had been sketchy with the details, other than that a man had been arrested after he'd held two men hostage, one of which had been Lenny, Scott's friend. I'd not wanted to imagine what had happened to either man, but I was sure it wasn't good given that they'd ended up in the hospital.

The intercom buzzed, pulling me from my worrisome thoughts. "Yes Sarah?"

"I've got a visitor here that you might want to make time for."

Her voice was full of humour and my heart skipped a beat. I was out of the chair and out of my office door before common sense could prevail. Scott stood next to Sarah's desk, looking all windswept with a smile on his face.

"Hey Baby. What are you doing here?" I asked, a goofy smile spreading over my face.

"I'm not needed in work until two, so I thought I'd come and see if I could interest you in a lunch date." His milky skin became a beautiful shade of pink as his gaze all but begged me to say yes.

It had been three days since I'd seen him. He'd been pulling double shifts to help out in one of the other restaurants, due to some staff being off sick.

"You have an hour before your next meeting," Sarah stated, before I could open my mouth to speak.

Her smug grin got an eye roll from me before I glanced back to Scott. "Looks like it's your lucky day."

"Every day is my lucky day with you," he muttered, as he stepped closer and hugged me.

At a loss how to respond with emotions balling in my throat, I wrapped my arms around him tightly and kissed the top of his silky head. The scent of limes filled my nose as he tucked his head into my neck, the way he loved to do. The weight of him against my body was perfect as he gave a contented sigh and nuzzled at my skin above my shirt collar.

The air in the room seemed to disappear as my feelings wanted to be set free. Every time we were together, I found it harder to contain the words that were desperate to pour from my lips. *Do it, just tell him how you feel.*

If only it were that easy.

It is, just do it.

God I wanted to be brave and take that step. My gaze met Sarah's and I was reminded I was not alone. Sarah remained silent, watching us with a lovey dovey expression on her face.

I eased back and lifted my hand to tilt Scott's head back so I could see his face. The look of adoration on his face was enough to derail my plans and I drew him back to me. My lips met his in a soft kiss full of promise. I wanted him to know how I felt, and if I couldn't give him the words right then, I'd give him what I could. As the need to pour all the emotions into the kiss flooded through me, my tongue moved along the seam of his lips, encouraging him to open for me. My hand moved to his throat, holding him still as I devoured his mouth.

As I tasted toothpaste and something sweet, he moaned and his body shook in my arms. The hand holding his throat tightened as his Adam's Apple bobbed.

Fuck who was watching, I needed him to know, he was it for me.

Relaxing the hand that held him, I pulled back when he ground harder against me and my cock tried to take charge. "We have to stop, Baby," I gasped and decided to look away from his puffy lips slick with my saliva.

"You don't have to stop on my account," came a cheeky female reply.

Doing my best to act like my face wasn't a blazing inferno of heat, I raised my brow and tilted my head in Sarah's direction. "Is that so?"

The bugger didn't show an ounce of shame as she kept staring at us. "I love a good show as much as the next person, and I have a feeling you two would set my knickers on fire."

My mouth hung open at her audacity, but Scott seemed to find it hilarious as he started to shake with laughter.

"Oh I like your assistant," he said, struggling to talk past the giggles.

"Yeah well, if she carries on like this she might not be my assistant for long," I quipped back, but without any real threat.

Her gaze went heavenward before she gave Scott a flirty wink. "I thought you two were going to... eat." Her eyes were alight with devilment as I choked at the true meaning I could hear in her voice as she said the word '*eat*'.

"God, you're incorrigible. How did I not know this about you?"

"You did, you just chose to ignore it. Anyway, having a debate about me is wasting your lunch break."

With that reminder, I tugged Scott to the door. Did we have time to find an empty room? As I pulled him towards the lift, his feet started to drag. As I glanced at his face, where there had been giddy excitement in the office, there was nothing but worry.

Stupid fucker.

I stopped and spun around. "Did you take the stairs to come up and see me?"

His eyes shifted to the lift halfway down the carpeted hallway, then back to me. "I took the... stairs."

The hesitation and glance back down the hallway forced me to move in the opposite direction. It was a pain to have to use the stairs as it would eat into our time together but his needs came first. And as much as I wouldn't mind being trapped in a lift with him, I had no supplies this time to help occupy our time. A sigh left my mouth before I could think to stop it.

Scott tugged his hand from mine as I opened the door to the top of the stairs. "You can get the lift if you want. I'll meet you at the bottom."

My forehead furrowed and I gave Scott an assessing look. "I didn't sigh because I have to take the stairs, I sighed because I have no supplies with me to encourage you to take the lift with me." As I spoke, his eyes brightened. It would seem I'd been right about him thinking I'd sighed because of having to use the stairs.

His face flushed and he glanced back at the lift through the open door. "Maybe you need to be better prepared Daddy for the next time I... come." With that, he turned and started down the stairs.

My mouth hung open for a full second before it closed and I gave chase to the giggling man who was now running down the stairs, encouraging me to chase him. Laughter filled the stairwell as I jogged after him, a grin stuck to my face at his playful behaviour. All the stress I usually felt at work seemed to disappear by the time I hit the bottom steps, panting.

"Oh Daddy, you need to be faster than that if you want to catch me," he stated, his chest heaving as he sucked in several breaths. His face was alight with humour as he put his hands on his hips and wagged his brows at me.

Ignoring that fact I was panting like a racehorse, I smirked. "You wait till the weekend. Daddy has ways and means to catch his boy." I wriggled my fingers and gave him my best Dick Dastardly impersonation.

"Dream on Daddy," he responded though when I glanced down, the bulge in his jeans said he was more than happy for whatever I planned to do to him.

"Come on, before I decide to start early." I took hold of his hand and dragged him to the door leading into the reception area when his eyes fired a challenge at me. The boy was bloody lethal, he could make me forget everything.

And that's a bad thing because?

I barely resisted rolling my eyes at the obvious answer… nothing.

Work, this is a workplace remember.

Chapter 11

Scott

The anticipation of the last few days made it impossible to continue to act like nothing was going on. With the thought of spending three uninterrupted days with Luke, my hands shook as I finished setting up the last table.

The shift had been long and busy, but with my concentration focused on what was going to happen the minute I got outside the building, I couldn't find it in me to complain. Not that I would have with everyone doing their best to put on a brave face after what had happened to Lenny on New Year's Eve.

Nathan had only allowed us to visit Lenny once he was out of the hospital. It had been shocking to see his bruised and battered face. He'd not gone into too much detail because there was going to be a court case sometime later in the year and he'd said he didn't want to be reminded of it. I didn't argue because I really wasn't sure I wanted to know all the details about him getting beat up by a wack job. A wack job who it turned out was the ex of one of the club subs, Ferron, who Lenny had befriended.

Ferron was a nice guy, if not a little timid. I'd only seen him briefly when I'd visited the club with Sawyer one time. Despite already downloading the App onto my phone, he'd felt guilty and decided we needed to go ask Nathan if it was okay. It didn't matter to me, I was grateful because I'd met Luke through the app. My stomach churned at the reality that I could have ended up with some weirdo.

Stop it, you found Luke, that's what counts.

Warmth spread through my chest at how, since New Year's Eve, things had been great between us. Well, bar the fact we hardly got any time together due to work and living on opposite sides of London. With the urge to whine wanting to take hold of me, I worked on reminding myself Luke was coming to collect me tonight and we had three whole days to spend together.

"Are you nearly done?" I span round fast at the sound of Theo's voice coming from the direction of the bar.

"Fuck man, you nearly frightened the life out of me." Clutching my chest, I giggled.

"Now that wouldn't do with your weekend plans of sex and debauchery." Theo smirked as he strolled towards me.

As he'd been the only one not telling me to dump Luke, he'd been the one I'd confided in about my ongoing relationship with him. I'd needed someone to talk to besides my mother, who was only too keen to ask me stuff she had no business knowing. A shudder ran through me at the interest she'd expressed when she'd accidentally heard me call Luke Daddy on the phone, the last time I'd been to visit her.

I'd had to do some evasive manoeuvres since then, but the text I'd got the day before said my time was running out. She'd invited Luke and me for Sunday lunch. As much as I wanted her to get to know Luke, I was also cautious as to what she might ask about what she'd overheard. Luke was still a little skittish at times when we were in public and around his work colleagues.

I shook off my worries. "It wouldn't, you're right. It's taken a lot of jiggling for us to get these days off together."

"What jiggling? And who's the us?" Adam asked as he appeared from the reception area. My heart sank that he might have overheard our conversation.

I gave Theo a beseeching look, which the fucker ignored and strolled off, leaving me to face Adam alone. My mind searched for an answer that seemed reasonable. My shoulders sagged. *Sod it.*

With that running through my head, I stood up straighter and met Adam's suspicious gaze. "Luke, he's been working hard to get us a couple of days off so we can spend some quality time together." There, I'd said it, and the world hadn't suddenly stopped turning.

When a thunderous expression started to appear on Adam's face, I wondered if I'd counted my eggs a little too soon.

I braced as his hand came up and he pointed at me.

"No way! Are you still dating that knob? I thought after that run-in last December, you had seen sense."

A sob rose up my throat and cut off my ability to respond. Tears sheened my eyes and all the happiness I'd been feeling bubbling inside me burst under the bitter edge to Adam's voice. His eyes narrowed on me and I struggled to speak.

As I took a deep breath, I recalled Luke's warm smile when I'd decided to visit him at work a few days back. I'd started to notice that whenever he looked at me, his face would light up. The knowledge that I could do that gave me the strength to swallow the ball of anxiety wanting to choke me. Finding my shoulders had slouched, I pushed them back and met Adam's hard stare with one of my own. "Listen, I understand you're concerned for me. I get it. But you don't know the Luke I do. He is *different* to the person he shows the world. He isn't the bastard you seem to think he is—"

"You thought he was a bastard," Adam pointed out, not letting me finish.

My teeth ground together as I reminded myself Adam was worried about me. "Yes I did. Now that I've got to know him, I don't feel that way anymore. Adam… I love him…" I trailed off, unsure who was more shocked by my confession, him or me.

Well, shit.

I'd known for a little while that what I felt for him was more than just a passing fancy. But until right then, until I'd said it aloud, I'd not put a name to the feelings that emerged every time I thought about him.

"Seriously, you love him." Adam's face conveyed a wealth of concern as his words struck me hard.

"I do, I love Luke." The conviction in my voice rang out and Adam's eyes widened but not on me. They were looking somewhere behind me at something else… at someone else. The hairs on the back of my neck stood up and I didn't need to move to know who was stood behind me. I could sense eyes boring into my back.

Whatever colour had been on my face a second before, drained away as I twisted around, my hands balled at my sides.

"Hey," I muttered, doing my level best not to stare at Luke's face when my suspicion was confirmed. He stood like a statue by the kitchen door.

"Hey yourself Baby. Are you ready to leave?" His voice sounded strained and forced me to look more closely at his face. There were deep grooves around his mouth and his brow was furrowed, but other than that there was no indication as to what he was thinking.

Was he upset about what I'd said?

Had he heard my confession?

When I couldn't find any answers, I looked at Adam. "I'm done right? I can go."

The tension in the room seemed to increase as Adam gave a stilted nod. His gaze moved to Luke then back to me, then his eyelashes lowered and shielded whatever he was thinking.

When wishing the floor would open up and swallow me whole didn't work, I marched to where Luke was stood. *Make a stand, he's your boyfriend. You just told Adam you love him. Prove it.*

Not needing any more spurring on, I took hold of the collar of Luke's jacket with both hands. As I tugged, I stood on my tiptoes until his mouth was in reach for me to kiss him. I gave him a second to register my intention, and when his eyes widened and his nostrils flared but he didn't move, I claimed his mouth in a hard kiss. The driving need behind the kiss was to know that we were okay, that my confession to Adam hadn't fucked things up and scared him off me.

It's too soon to be talking about love.

Who said so?

With the urge to argue with myself wanting to derail me from the kiss, I poured all the frustration into fuelling it instead.

A growl rumbled up Luke's chest right as his arms came around my shoulders dragging me against his firm body. His chest rose and fell in quick succession as he took control of the kiss, making me release a needy groan.

So lost in the feel of his mouth on mine, it took a second to register Carl's booming voice. "Is Scott trying to take a leaf out of our book, Adam?"

Luke's head lifted first and his gaze met mine, promising me that we weren't finished, before it shifted to the men stood watching us.

A shiver rippled down my body, responding to the desire I'd seen in his dark eyes.

The tension I'd felt earlier seemed to mount as Luke released me and stepped back as he confronted Carl and Adam.

"Evening Luke." Carl nodded his head and his hand took hold of Adam's, as if trying to tether Adam's vibrating body to his side.

The conversation was stilted before I managed to tug Luke out the back door. After running to get my coat and the bag I'd packed for the weekend at his home, and stowing them in the boot of Luke's car, I released a pent up breath. I hated being unable to tell whether I'd fucked things up and would be unpacking my bag back at my flat, instead of at Luke's home.

"Whatever's got you chewing on your lip like that?" The husky question and the warm fingers tugging my lip from my teeth pulled my gaze to Luke.

"Do you really want to know?"

His face lost the teasing quality as his fingers went to my chin and held it as his gaze searched my face. "Always, Baby."

"Did you hear me?" I asked in a breathy rush, my own eyes locked on his to see what his reaction was. The air in the car seemed to disappear as a smile spread over his face and a buzzing started in my ears.

"Did I hear what, Baby?" he teased, his smile seeming to grow bigger, if that was possible.

"You're gonna make me say it, aren't you!" I sighed and then huffed when he chuckled.

His mouth lowered to mine and his tongue teased my lower lip. "It would be nice for you to say it to me and not to someone else, yes." His hot breath merged with mine before he moved back a fraction.

With a groan of complaint at him pulling away, I pouted. "Daddy, you're not playing fair." His eyes remained on me, causing my pulse to skyrocket at what I could see in their depth. Driven by the need to give him what he asked for, for what his eyes begged for, I met his lips with mine. "I love you. I love you so much Daddy. I'm sorry I said it to someone else first," I confessed against his mouth. My eyes closed at hearing how needy I sounded.

Chapter 12

Luke

I'd thought I was going to lose my shit when I'd stepped into the restaurant to find Scott confessing his love for me. I'd had to forcibly lock my knees to stop them from shaking and giving away how much he'd rocked me to my core.

With my heart still trying to figure out what rate was best, there was a buzzing in my ears. This increased after hearing the tail end of the conversation between Luke and Adam.

I'd been at a loss, so I'd stood like a bloody fool, my feet refusing to move. Then Scott had stomped across the room and I'd been sucked into a vacuum of emotions at the determination etched into his face.

Whatever had happened to my fight or flight instinct at that moment, fuck only knew, but now we were in the car the instinct to fight reared up with such vengeance my body shook.

"I love you." Scott muttered against my mouth repeatedly when I became immobilised, then his eyelashes drifted down.

Painfully swallowing the lump in my throat, I cupped Scott's cheeks. "Open your eyes. I need you to look at me." When he did as I asked, my fingers trembled. "I love you. I've known for a while. I was just waiting for the right moment." His eyes welled with tears but his face beamed with a happiness that caught my breath. His lips parted and I shook my head. "Let me finish, please. Hearing you say you love me was one of those moments you want to capture and tuck away, just so you can pull it out and look at when you're feeling low. This is why I want you to say it to my face, so I can always remember the first time you said you love me when you were looking at me." There was heat creeping up my face by the time I'd finished being all sappy, although I didn't care, because I wanted him to understand what the moment meant to me, to us.

His chin wobbled and a tear slid down his cheek. He blinked several times before he leant forward and laid his forehead against mine. His watery gaze held mine. "I love you, Luke. You give me rainbows on a rainy day. You give me so much joy, sometimes I have to pinch myself to remind me that this is real." He hiccuped and gave me a sheepish smile. "I'm sorry that you heard me say I love you—"

I placed a finger over his mouth, stopping him from speaking. "Don't say you wish I'd not heard you because I'm so happy I did." My mouth lowered to his and I captured his lips in a sweet kiss. "Let's go back to mine, we're wasting our precious time together." I gave him a sexy sneer that earned me a low moan.

"Then drive Daddy," he said, while pushing me back into my seat.

As I chuckled, I switched on the ignition and did as I was told. Scott chatted excitedly as I drove through the dark streets, doing my best to focus on the road and him. By the time we got to my home he was all but bouncing in his seat. "You seem pretty excited."

While his hand went to his seatbelt, his gaze met mine. "Oh please, three whole days with no… interruptions." His face clouded with doubt as he hesitated and my jaw bunched.

"Why the hesitation, Baby? Am I missing something?" My stomach twisted into knots as he shifted his gaze out the window.

"My mum invited us for Sunday dinner."

As I started to relax, his next words removed that feeling faster than lightning could light a sky.

"She overheard me calling you Daddy, and I think she's going to want me to explainaboutit," he finished in a rush, the words mashing together. His face still remained averted as I worked to figure out how I felt about this.

Would his mother accept this part of our relationship? *Would she push Scott to dump me?*

That thought caused my hands to clench until my fingernails dug into my palm. As I inhaled, I hoped it would stop me from jumping the gun. "Are you worried about the pressure they'll put on you to leave me?"

His head twisted to me so fast he was a blur for a second. His face was contorted into a mask of horror. "I'm not dumping you for anybody! My parents are the most understanding people I've ever met. I'm just saying that there could be questions that might make you uncomfortable if we go to lunch with them. My mum would never have invited you into our home if she thought there was something bad going on between us, I swear." A sob was stifled by his fist being rammed between his lips.

I got out of the car and was around the bonnet in seconds. I had the door open and was lifting him out of the seat before he could protest. I held him tightly. "Okay. It's okay. We'll go to lunch and whatever questions your mum has I'll answer them." I hoped like hell Scott didn't notice the nerves in my voice.

His head lifted and his tear-stained face came into view. "We'll answer them. We are a team Daddy, you and me. Got it?" he growled, not sounding at all menacing.

There was such determination on his face I was compelled to agree with him. We were in this together. *No more hiding, remember.*

"I love you." The emotions whelmed up as he gave me a watery smile. Every time I spoke the words, the feelings that came with them wanted me to acknowledge them.

"I love you too, Daddy." With that he wiggled out of my arms and stepped back, then he took hold of my hand. "Let's get my bag. You never know what treats I might have brought with me," he giggled.

A shiver raced down my spine and I struggled to pull my thoughts away from thoughts of lace and silk. "You're going to pay for teasing me, you know that right?"

"With the paddle, Daddy?" he asked, his voice full of excitement.

The narrowed stare I gave caused him to laugh harder as he pulled me to the boot of the car. Once the bag was retrieved, I locked the car and we made our way inside. The warmth of the house blanketed us as Scott deposited his bag on the stairs.

Walking down the hallway, I glanced back. "Do you want a glass of wine?"

He nodded before I carried on down the hallway to the kitchen with the sound of his steps behind me. Scott walked over to take a seat in his favourite spot, right by the window, overlooking the garden. I'd discovered Scott loved the outdoors, but the sun, he advised wasn't his friend. It made his lily-white skin red and blister before it went back to being pale.

There was a companionable silence as I retrieved the wine from the fridge, making sure it was the one Scott liked. During the time he'd spent in my home, I'd started to discover what his likes and dislikes were. After pouring wine into two glasses, I went to the table to deposit them, before sitting next to Scott.

He yawned as he picked up the wine, then gave me a sheepish grin. "Sorry, it's been a long week and all the extra shifts are catching up with me."

"Listen, I've no expectations my sweet boy. I'm just looking forward to spending more than a couple of hours with you. I don't care what we do." His brows rose and heat spread up his neck as he fired me a look of disbelief. I chuckled. "Okay, I'll rephrase that. I want to get you naked and ravish your body for hours… but we have days for me to do that. For now, let's go chill in front of the TV with our wine and snuggle on the couch."

I was rewarded with a big smile as he got up and held out the hand not holding his wine glass. I took it and within minutes I found myself sat on the sofa, Scott's head in my lap.

He'd fallen asleep almost immediately he'd plonked his head on my thighs and demanded I stroke his hair. While I continued to gently stroke the silky strands, I stared down at his unguarded face, unable to ignore the age difference I tried daily not to think about.

He stirred for a moment, and I realised my hand had stilled. Resuming my gentle touches, he settled quickly.

But the contented feeling it gave me didn't stop my worry. Will the age gap be a problem in the future?

It was what I'd been avoiding asking myself, especially when I didn't like what the possible answer would be.

No one can predict the future. Stop seeking trouble where there is none.

I'd not been stupid enough not to notice the glances we'd received from others when we'd been out together. Sometimes I could ignore them easily when Scott gave me one of his incredible smiles, but other times I had to force myself not to run for the hills and hide. It was a mind fuck. I'd talked about it with Brett and his comment of "Rome wasn't built in a day," ran through my mind. I sighed softly, trying not to disturb Scott as my fingers continued to stroke his hair.

Questions about our future worked to undo the calm feeling Scott's presence usually gave me, while the film I wasn't watching played in the background.

I laid my head back on the cushion and shut my eyes. *He loves me. He loves me.* The litany continued and I held onto it like an anchor tethering a boat in a storm. I prayed that the anchor could hold us through whatever storms we were going to meet. Because something told me the simple declaration of our mutual feelings wasn't going to be enough to weather every storm.

I told you, stop borrowing trouble. Love can conquer all, it can.

If there was an edge of desperation to the voice in my head, I ignored it and forced myself to focus on the here and now. Something, unfortunately, I wasn't all that good at.

Chapter 13

Scott

The scent of Luke's aftershave wafted around me as the solid pillow under my head shifted. I opened my blurry eyes to peer down at the smooth chest I was nestled against. A smile spread over my face, making my cheeks ache. The weight of the arms on my back tightened and I nuzzled at the warm skin under me. That resulted in a chuckle rumbling up Luke's chest, dislodging my head.

"What?" I asked. Still half asleep, I couldn't figure out why Luke was laughing as I eyed the foolish grin on his face.

"Your bristly chin was tickling me," he answered, with laughter in his voice.

I wiped at my sleepy eyes. Was Luke ticklish? A mischievous idea popped into my head and I hid my smirk and lowered my head, before purposefully nuzzling at him to see what he'd do next. The laughter increased as he moved to try and get my face away from his chest.

My man is ticklish, how did I not know this?

With him still trying to escape, my hands lowered to his sides and I dug my fingers in, tickling him.

"Hey, not fair... stop that," he roared past the laughter as he worked harder to stop me.

My own laughter mixed with his as we wrestled over the bed, panting and giggling as I clung on like a limpet, my fingers making him howl with laughter until tears leaked out of his eyes.

"You'll pay for this," he panted as he shifted in one direction then quickly changed to the other, fooling me and allowing him to roll on top of me.

I sucked in a breath at the feel of his erection now pressing against my own. His mouth moved to mine before I could exhale and the air remained trapped in my lungs as he devoured my mouth.

I had a vague recollection of Luke carrying me to bed and stripping me off the night before, before I fell into an exhausted sleep. With a seed of disappointment that I'd wasted our first night together wanting to take root, I opened my mouth, allowing his tongue to sweep inside and take control of the kiss.

A groan of protest was pulled from me as Luke lifted his head, only for it to die as his lips and teeth attacked my neck. He licked and sucked at the tender flesh of my throat as he thrusted his hips. His erection pressed firmly against mine and the pre-cum leaking from our cocks allowed them to glide in a sensual rub against each other. Delicious sensations spread through my cock, my testicles and down into my clenching backside. With the need to feel his cock inside me firmly in the driving seat, I begged, "Please Daddy, fuck me."

The lips that had reached my chest disappeared and Luke's heavy-lidded gaze met mine. "Oh God yes, Baby boy." His chest heaved as he crawled up my body. He balanced on one arm, still caging me in as he reached towards the bedside cabinet that housed his supplies.

As his body hovered over mine, his cock leaked and my mouth watered for a taste. Before I could overthink it, I shimmied down the mattress between his spread legs. The head of his cock bobbed in front of my face and I tongued the veiny head. The taste was all too brief as Luke moaned and rolled away.

"What did you do that for," I whined in protest, as I struggled to untangle myself from the duvet that had shifted with Luke, and trapped me.

His finger tapped at my nose as his eyes sparkled with joy. "I won't last two minutes if you put those pretty lips around me."

"And? I don't see an issue with that Daddy." I twitched my nose, dislodging his finger.

"Aren't you the one that just demanded that I fuck you?" His dark brows rose and I found I couldn't argue with him, so I clamped my lips together in a pout.

When all that got was a hard stare, I brought out the big guns and fluttered my eyelashes, giving him my best 'woe is me' expression. I didn't have the opportunity to celebrate at the exasperated sigh he released, because he pounced on me. His mouth took mine in a brutal kiss that left me achingly hard.

There was a feeling of fingers against my pucker as he rolled and pulled me on top of him, his mouth not releasing mine. I spread my legs, desperate to move things along. The feel of his cock pressing against my flesh felt like a hot brand. My skin tingled and I ground down, needing more.

As a dry finger breached me, the burn caused a moan to leave my mouth. My chest heaved as I struggled with the need to take a breath and the need to carry on kissing Luke. The need for air won out and I lifted my head, gasping as my body trembled.

Hot lips didn't give me a second to catch my breath as they moved down my throat. Luke removed his finger from my arse and his hand disappeared as he shifted across the mattress. It took a second to register the click of a lid opening for it to sink in what he was doing.

Wet fingers returned to my backside and slid over my sensitive hole, awakening every nerve ending as Luke teased me. Lube was gently rubbed into my flesh until my hips were lifting and pushing back. Two fingers eased past the tight rim of muscles and the burning sensation I love so much swept through me. I arched back and pushed down wanting more, needing something to stop the desperation clawing at me.

"Fuck me Daddy, fuck me nowwww," I pleaded, as his fingers stretched me and a third was added, stuffing my channel full. Yet still, it wasn't enough. "Now Daddy, I'm ready, pleaseeeeee."

A heartfelt sigh was released as I was lifted up into a sitting position so Luke could put on the condom that he'd placed on the bed cover. His hands shook and my mouth dried at the aroused cock he rolled the condom down. Luke's gaze pinned me in place the second he was cloaked, as if he'd known I was planning to just jump on him.

As he moved to sit me on his lap, I trembled. His cock was trapped against me as he tugged me closer to him. "I get to decide when my pretty boy. I know you want me to fuck you, but I want to make love to you." His words were whispered against my mouth and my heart soared. The edge of desperation abated at hearing the love in his voice, and on seeing it reflected in his eyes.

"Oh Daddy, yes," I replied through a breathy moan.

He helped me to move up onto my knees and then carefully lowered me down. The head of his cock brushed against my sensitive skin and made me wish that we didn't have to use a condom. The thought fled as he breached me and the burn turned into pleasure. The stretch was unbelievable and my eyes crossed as large hands held onto my hips, guiding me up and down in a slow, torturous rhythm. It was too much, but not nearly enough, and my cock throbbed painfully as it brushed against Luke's abs.

His hazel eyes darkened and held my gaze. The love in their depths was doing a number on me, my moans filled the air as he drove me higher and higher with each thrust and hip roll. He tilted his hips and moved me, and I groaned at the feel of his cock brushing over my prostate.

My eyes rolled into the back of my head as he did it again and again. As I trembled and shook with need, my hand lowered to my cock.

"No Baby, that's Daddy's."

With that, my hand was knocked away. Before I could complain, warm fingers clasped my cock firmly and stroked in time to the cock thrusting into my arse. Sweat beaded on my forehead and my hair stuck to it. Luke was faring no better, his face shining in the light pouring through the window.

The focus on his face was my undoing. The rapt attention was like a sensual kiss to my whole body and my cock jerked hard as it rejoiced. Hot cum hit my stomach as Luke continued to assault my body with pleasure. His intense gaze caused my heart to soar, making it impossible to take a decent breath.

His mouth slammed against mine as my cock continued to thrum with pleasure. The cock in my arse hardened and swelled, making it feel impossibly large as Luke thrust up once more and released a strangled moan into my mouth. His body froze as his cock pulsed and once again I felt disappointed that we were using a condom, which stopped me from feeling his cum.

I swallowed his moans and swept my tongue along his. Then I sucked his tongue into my mouth, mimicking what I liked to do to his cock, needing to prolong his pleasure.

After what felt like endless minutes, he finally released my mouth. Our chests heaved as he collapsed back onto the mattress, huffing and puffing faster than a freight train. His arms kept me imprisoned against his slick chest as hot breaths ghosted over my neck and face.

"That's how to exercise in the morning," I gasped breathlessly.

"I'm sure going to the gym would be safer. I think you were trying to kill me," he mumbled, not opening his eyes as I lifted my head to see if he was serious. Seeing as his lips were tilted up and he looked like the cat who'd got all the cream, I didn't argue.

"Are you saying I'll have to wait for round two?" I asked, tongue in cheek. I couldn't hold the laughter in as I was rolled over onto my back, cold cum smearing my stomach. Luke's cloaked cock slipped from my arse and left me feeling empty.

"Round two... are you saying you weren't satisfied with round one?"

Although there was humour dancing in his eyes, there was also something else that caused my chest to tighten. "I'm greedy Daddy. Why, when you can blow my mind like that, would I not want more?" I offered up my lips and breathed a sigh of relief as he took them in a gentle kiss.

"I see, you're saying I've created a nymphomaniac?" He chuckled as his mouth moved to the corner of my lips and he nibbled.

"Yes, Daddy. It's *all your* fault," I moaned as he continued to tease me. The weight of his body pinning me to the bed, even after the mind-blowing orgasm, gave my cock ideas as it started to plump.

"Ohh, we're playing the blame game. Are you being a naughty boy trying to push the responsibility on to me?" he whispered, right before his tongue swept along the seam of my lips.

As I panted and trembled, I got a distinct feeling I wasn't the only one enjoying the teasing. Wanting to see if I was right, I pushed my hips up and ground my now solid erection against him.

"Oh fuck Baby," he gasped as his hips met my thrust. "Shower... let's take this to the bathroom."

I'm not sure how we made it to the bathroom and in the shower without doing ourselves an injury, as Luke couldn't keep his hands off me, but we did.

The hot water sluiced over my back as I knelt on the hard tiled floor and sucked Luke's cock to the back of my throat a few minutes later. The steam filled the cubicle, along with Luke's groans. The sound of the water was drowned out by the pleasure buzzing through me when cum filled my mouth and leaked down my chin. All the while, my hand jerked my cock till cum spurted over my thighs. Breathless, my body shook with exhaustion as I released Luke's cock and laid my head against his wet, hairy leg. "That's how to start the day," I mumbled through my swollen lips.

"Ain't that the truth," Luke rasped.

As I glanced up at him through wet eyelashes and met his heavy-lidded stare, I exhaled at the emotions I could see in their hazel depths. *How had I got so lucky?*

Chapter 14

Luke

"Hello," Scott shouted as we entered through the front door, alerting his parents to our arrival. I barely resisted the urge to fidget when Scott's mother, Megan, appeared out of the room she'd ushered me into on New Year's Eve.

With the sound of the door closing behind me, sweat slid down my spine. *Why had I agreed to this? Because you're blindly in love with Scott, that's why, now get over yourself.*

The man in question took hold of my hand and tugged me away from the door and down the hallway to the woman that was giving me a speculative stare.

It's going to be alright, it is.

Clutching Scott's hand tightly, I lifted the bag I held in my other hand and offered it to Megan. At the party she'd insisted I call her by her first name, and though I wasn't entirely comfortable with it, I'd not argued with her.

The bag I held out was taken, and Megan gave me an odd stare that I couldn't interpret, before she opened the bag. Scott had said we didn't need to bring anything with us, but I wanted to start off on the right foot, so I'd bought a bottle of champagne, a box of chocolates and a small house plant.

"Oh, this is lovely. How thoughtful of you, Luke," she gushed as she rooted in the bag. A smile too much like Scott's lit her face as she glanced back at us. "I wasn't expecting anything, but this is a lovely surprise. We can have the wine with lunch, but I'm keeping the chocolates to myself or this one will eat them all before I get a look in." She pointed to Scott and gave a mock glare. Then she clutched the bag to her body as if to protect the contents.

"There's no need to go on mum, I'm not that bad," he chuckled. "You're acting like you don't get gifts or something."

"Those are normally on my birthday or Christmas so they don't count," she said chastising Scott, but with humour dancing in her gaze.

He released my hands and went to wrap his arms around her, hardly giving her time to move the bag out of the way. "You know that I'm the best gift ever. So why would I need to give you anything else other than my sparkling wit and presence. Seriously, there's no competition."

There was the sound of a smack as she cuffed Scott around the ear, making him holler and pull away. "Hey, what have I told you about hitting children? I'll have to report you to social services if this carries on." He giggled, rubbing at his ear.

"I'm sure Luke does more than that to you when you're his *naughty boy* and I bet you don't threaten him with social services." Her face flushed as the words left her mouth, but she laughed at the pair of us when we both froze.

There had to be a similar expression on both our faces as I caught Scott's mouth hanging open and the deep flush riding up his neck and face. Mine felt like it could heat a large room as I struggled to decide where to look. Any thoughts of sitting down and eating went out the window with the implication of what she'd meant weighing like a lead ball in my stomach.

"Mum, did you have to go there?" Scott whined, a scowl causing his mother to snigger which, for some reason, released a little of the tightness holding my stomach hostage.

"I'm sorry it just sort of slipped out?" She gave me a conspiratorial wink that left me struggling not to see the funny side of it when Scott stamped his foot.

I bit my lip to stop the smile from spreading over my face when Scott glanced at me accusingly. "You better not be taking her side Daddy."

The smile I'd had disappeared at the sudden tension filling Scott, who had gone deathly pale. His face fell and his eyes gleamed with panic. Clearly he'd not meant to call me 'Daddy' in front of his mother. I wasn't sure how I felt after her teasing. *Did it matter what she thought?*

Before I could overthink it and follow Alice down the rabbit hole, I took a couple of steps, closing the distance separating Scott and me. I took hold of him and pretended his mother wasn't stood less than a few feet from us.

"I might have been, but who could blame me, it was funny Baby." I gave a strained laugh, willing Scott to see that I wasn't cross with him for outing me so spectacularly. "Your mum has you pegged."

I winked at him and glanced at his mother, who looked concerned more than disgusted by what her son had said. "Your son can be a little bit of a handful, right? But he's in safe hands with me, I know how to make him behave." The jokey tone I used seemed to release a little of the tension in the hallway. Scott rolled his eyes at me when I glanced back at him, but there was gratitude in their depth as his gaze shifted to his mother.

Before Scott could say anything, Megan gave him a smile of reassurance. "I'm sorry, sweetheart. I was messing with you." She stepped to us and rubbed at Scott's arm, giving me a beaming smile that left me feeling both grateful and humbled. "That will teach me right? Speaking before I can engage my brain."

"Who hasn't engaged their brain?" came the question from behind us. Scott's dad, James, peered out of the living room, his eyes crinkling as he glanced between Megan and us. "Did you put your foot in it again?"

He gave an exaggerated sigh when Megan nodded. "Woman, when will you ever learn?" His tone, though exasperated, held a depth of love.

The strain of moments ago melted away entirely as we were guided into the dining room and James chatted as he indicated where we should sit.

Sat around the pine table, the conversation was thankfully switched to Scott's promotion and his move to The Flamingo bar and restaurant as the head waiter. With the wine flowing, Megan mellowed and I found myself relaxing as I listened to Scott banter with his parents.

Had I ever had a meal like this with my parents? Had there ever been this easy camaraderie between us?

If there was, I couldn't recall it. If anything, when anyone had spoken during meal times, it had been stilted and boring conversation that only skimmed the surface and held no depth.

Scott's parents could never be accused of that, they were open… maybe a little too much, but their love for their son was unmistakable. When he'd explained that they were very liberal, I'd thought he'd exaggerated, yet as I sat listening to them now, the truth of his words sank home.

The little incident in the hallway seemed forgotten, and as I searched Megan's face, I realised that she wasn't acting any different to when I'd first met her. If anything, she was more relaxed now than she had been on New Year's Eve.

Was it possible that what Scott and I did together made no difference to her?

As the afternoon wore on, we moved from the dining room, into the lounge and settled on the sofa for coffee and cake.

When Scott rested against me, I automatically took the hand he offered and laced my fingers with his. He nestled his head on my shoulder and released a sigh of contentment which gave me a warm glow. I loved how comfortable he was in his own skin, how he didn't care about what anyone thought about his behaviour towards me. Years I'd held back a part of me, yet with Scott, the need to shield who I really was disappeared.

My eyebrows met as my brow furrowed. When had the aching loneliness that had been my constant companion disappeared? Having lived with it for forever, it took several minutes of concentration for it to sink in how tranquil I felt. The ache I'd got so used to being in my chest… was gone. In its place was something warm, vibrant and life-affirming: Scott.

My fingers tightened on his as emotions swirled inside me and my heart lodged in my throat. The cushions shifted on the sofa and I glanced at Scott. His eyes were pools of concern and I realised I hadn't hidden my feelings. "Are you ready to go home?" His quiet question barely penetrated through the sound of my pulse hammering in my ears.

I'm not sure how I managed to act like nothing was wrong as Scott ushered us out of the house in record time and into the car. I sat for a second, trying to gather myself as both

Scott's parents' stood in the doorway, beaming and waving at us.

Would my parents' have been this nice to Scott? I nearly scoffed aloud at the obvious answer… no.

It doesn't matter.

Even as the thought registered, I knew deep inside that it did. I'd always sought my father's approval and though he was dead, there was still a part of me that needed to know that he accepted me, accepted who I really was.

With how Scott's parents had been with him, been with me, still running through my mind, I started the engine. Giving my full attention to the road, I avoided looking at Scott, whose gaze I felt like a weight against me.

A heavy silence filled the car as I drove through the light traffic. By the time we reached my home, I was convinced it matched the sombreness of my feelings. How do I explain how I feel? Would Scott understand, with his parents being so different?

Questions continued to pound at my skull as I drove up my drive and parked, still no closer to finding any answers.

Out of the car, I waited for Scott to follow. His feet dragged on the ground and he kept his gaze averted. Willing myself to keep it together, I tried to remember the tranquil feelings he gave me as I unlocked the front door, letting him pass before entering the house. After shutting the door, I stilled as I turned to face Scott.

He stood not more than a few feet from me, and it struck me how alive my home felt with him in it. How he took away the emptiness that seemed to make my home feel like an empty shell.

The house faded away as I took in the misery on his face, the pain I'd put there, by acting like a dick. Across the carpeted floor in a second, I wrapped my arms around his body. As I buried my nose in his scented hair, I inhaled and exhaled twice before I loosened my grip so I could tilt his head back and look at his face. A face filled with uncertainty and what looked like sorrow.

My breath hitched as emotions swirled and danced through me erratically, like an uncoordinated dancer. "God, I love you so much. But am I enough for you—"

"Of course you are," he all but growled as his hands came up and took a firm grip of my face. "I love you Daddy, nothing is going to change that. What set you off in my parents' house?" His hands trembled against my face.

As I tried to pull back, his fingers clung on to me. "Please tell me?"

His eyes implored me and I lowered my forehead until it rested on his, sighing in defeat. "My parents, as I've explained are...were, nothing like yours. It just brought it home to roost today, seeing your parents so accepting." With my increasing frustration, I tugged free and lifted my head, needing a moment.

The hurt on Scott's face sliced at my heart. My hands balled into fists as I swung around and stamped down the hall. *Alcohol, I need some alcohol.* I'd had a half a glass of wine with dinner because I'd been driving but now I needed some of the hard stuff.

No, you need to grow a pair of balls.

Not listening to the voice that sounded way too much like Brett, I marched to the cupboard the alcohol was stored in. As I grabbed a bottle of Scotch, a hand touched my arm gently.

"Daddy, talk to me."

The softly spoken demand cut through the layer of sadness wanting to suck me under and I withdrew my empty hand from the cupboard. I swallowed and met Scott's gaze.

Be brave for Scott, for you. You need to be honest.

With that conviction running through me, I took hold of Scott's hand with shaky fingers. "Why would you want to be with someone that comes from an emotionally stunted family? Who is emotionally stunted for fucksake! Why?" I growled in frustration.

Chapter 15

Scott

The harder I tried to figure out what had gone wrong at my parents, the more frustrated I'd become. So I'd stayed silent in the car, giving Luke the time to figure out how to talk about what was bothering him. These last few months, I'd come to understand that Luke was a deep thinker. He liked to work through things before he spoke about them. Although it was annoyingly frustrating to wait, I'd learned that pushing only made him worse.

Now though, I wondered if I shouldn't have pushed him a little sooner to talk about his real feelings about his father. Oh he'd talked about him, about the way he wanted Luke to act and behave, but we'd never talked about how he felt about it.

Luke had given away more than he probably realised at my parents. I'd not missed the look of longing that crossed his face more than once, when he'd watched my parents laughing and joking with me. As I'd never known them to be any different, it was hard for me to see how they were through Luke's eyes. Did it make a difference to him that I'd had a happy childhood?

His fingers tightened on mine and as they shook, I masked my own worries. Instead I gave him an encouraging smile.

"Talk to me," I begged, yet again.

"I… it's hard to explain, not without sounding like I'm jealous of what you've got," he muttered, his gaze moving to the floor.

"Daddy, look at me." Only when he glanced up did I carry on. "I get it… okay maybe not quite." I added when his brows rose. "My parents are unique, and I know I'm a lucky bastard to have them. I get your father wasn't like mine, but a wise person once said that we are what our parents create, but what we remain is up to us. You show me time and time again that you've changed, that you aren't the man your father wanted you to be. That might be hard to think about when you loved your father, but it's not wrong to be the man you want to be." Seeing a flicker of hope cross his face, I carried on, needing him to understand he was different, and that was okay.

"I think you need to talk to your mum about how you feel. It might help you move on and put the past to rest. We can't live in the past, we need to live in the here and now." I pointed between us. "This right here is what is important, not my or your parents. It's what we are building together that counts." I ended on a choked sob as I watched a tear slide down his pale cheek.

"How did you get so wise?" he rasped, his voice sounding decidedly gritty.

With the hope that we'd passed the crisis, I took the step that separated us and released his hand to wrap my arms around his waist. I tucked my head into his shoulder as his arms enfolded me. "I was born wise, so my mother said. Though I think she likes to add 'arse' to the end of the wise. I've no clue why."

His chest rumbled with laughter and his arms tightened. The tension that had been holding my shoulder blades hostage released, allowing them to slide back down to where they should have been.

"I'm not sure that talking to my mother will help… but I'll give it a go. Maybe it will help me understand my father more." He heaved a sigh and rested his chin on top of my head.

"I'll come with you if you like? We could go see her tomorrow if you want?" Even though the offer was genuine, I prayed he'd say no. The idea of spending our last day together talking to his mother did not fill me with enthusiasm.

"My mother's on a cruise with friends. She isn't due back for several weeks."

I tried to hide my relief.

"I love you," Luke chuckled, right next to my ear. His hot breath caused a shiver to race down my spine. "But you'll need to try harder if you want to mask your relief."

"You're not funny," I snorted indignantly, glaring up at him as I pulled back.

"Then let's see if I can change your mind on that."

Before I could figure out what he was going to do, he crouched and threw me over his shoulder. The air left my body as he headed for the hallway and up the stairs. By the time we reached the top step my cock had woken up to the idea of the fun times ahead.

What Luke didn't know was that I'd got dressed up in anticipation of coming home and spending a lazy Sunday afternoon in bed. When his mood had dipped, I'd thought that I'd not be getting a chance to share my little surprise. Now, as I wriggled in his arms, my cheeks flamed recalling precisely what I had on under my top and trousers.

A giggle bubbled up, then another. As I was dropped onto the bed, the mattress depressed and I bounced once. My laughter increased at the genuine smile developing on Luke's face.

"Do you think this is funny, do you? Maybe I need to go and get my paddle." There was a dark desire in his gaze as it swept over me.

The threat was laughable, with my cock jerking in the confines of my trousers at the idea of feeling the paddle against my silk-clad bottom. With that running through my mind, I sat up and pulled off my jacket. Throwing it on the floor, I took my time unbuttoning my shirt.

A light dawned in Luke's hazel eyes as they lowered to my hands and the vivid red lacy crop top came into view. His chest started to heave with each button I released.

"Did you get dressed up for me?" he growled. His large hands clenched at his sides as his jaw bunched.

With the knowledge of how aroused Luke got when I teased him, I finished unbuttoning my shirt and slipped it off to reveal the lacy top that hugged my torso like a second skin. I bent forward and took off my boots, dropping them to the floor along with my socks. There was a sharp inhale as my stocking-clad feet came into view.

I sat back, meeting Luke's heated stare as my hands moved to the button on my jeans. With the button open, my fingers tugged the zip down and this time, I could see Luke's reaction to the red garter and silky panties I wore underneath my trousers. His eyes became dark pools of lust as his breathing became choppy, but he held himself back.

As I wriggled my hips to push my trousers down my legs and reveal the lacy topped black stockings, I thought I'd broken his tight control as his whole body juddered. Yet he managed to remain standing at the end of the bed, only his hungry gaze devouring me.

Oh, that will not do.

I wanted him to break free of the control that he held far too tightly most of the time. With that in mind, I lowered my eyelashes, giving him a seductive smile as the trousers plopped to the floor and my legs were freed. I lay back on the black bed cover, knowing that I'd make quite the picture with my milky white skin, tattooed thighs, black stockings and the vivid red of my sexy underwear. The sheer hosiery gave my legs a shapely appearance, so I moved them to show them off.

The silky fabric stretched over my erection darkened as my cock pulsed and leaked with the feel of Luke's burning gaze sweeping my body. It felt like a caress to my nipples and they pebbled, pushing against the lacy top I wore.

"You look spectacular, Baby," he hissed through his teeth, as his gaze continued to roam over every inch of me.

"Thank you Daddy, but what are you doing all the way over there?" I pouted, after licking at my lips. I patted the bed next to me and fluttered my eyelashes at him.

"I want to look my fill Baby."

His voice sounded strained as his hands moved to strip off his own clothes. His hands faltered as I spread my legs and I sucked a finger into my mouth. When it was dripping wet I lowered it and let it slide down between my spread thighs to the silk barely covering my hole. I eased the silk away from my pucker, revealing my second secret.

I swallowed the chuckle that wanted to escape at the loud growl that came from Luke when he caught sight of the small plug I had inserted before we'd left the house. I wanted to be ready when we got home, but now I wasn't sure if I'd maybe taken it a step too far as his eyes glazed over.

The sound of cloth ripping met my ears and Luke's remaining clothes were left in a torn heap at his feet. He was on me before I could take a breath, his mouth devouring mine in a wet, hungry kiss that left me deaf and blind to everything but him. The taste of him flooded my mouth as his tongue slid over mine, before sucking it into his mouth. As our tongues met in a sensual duel, his body pressed mine into the bed. His pelvis pinned my lower body, stopping me from grinding against him and I mewled into his mouth.

"You want Daddy to lose control, don't you?" he rasped against the skin of my neck as his teeth raked over the flesh, causing my body to shiver and shudder against the cotton beneath me.

How did he expect me to form words?

I grunted instead as his hands seemed to be everywhere, touching me as they traced the lace and silk lovingly, driving my need higher. The lace rubbed at my skin, leaving tingling shivers to course through me. Hot breath was the only warning I got as Luke's mouth moved to my pebbled nipple, sucking it through the lace. I keened as my cock leaked against the silk holding it captive. The silky material tortured me, right along with Luke's hot mouth.

"Daddy..." I cried as he bit down hard on my nipple, a throbbing ache filling my chest and spreading pleasure through me. My body writhed against Luke's, seeking more. I made nonsensical noises as Luke took me apart with his mouth and his hands.

His firm body slid down mine, trapping my cock as he took his time exploring my lace-clad body. By the time he reached my silk panties, I didn't think I could hold on a moment longer, my cock achingly hard.

As I struggled to lift my head from the damp pillow to see why he'd stopped, my chest heaved. My hands dug into the duvet at how his hungry gaze was riveted to the silk garter belt and panties which were now several shades darker, soaked with pre-cum.

"It's a bloody good job I had no clue what you had on under your clothes today. I'd never have been able to keep a sensible thought in my head," he stated in a husky voice that did nothing to help my leaking cock.

It bucked, as if trying to get closer to the mouth that wasn't nearly close enough to my cock for my liking. "Please Daddy, stop teasing me," I begged, while attempting to lift my hips so he'd get the hint. His hot breath hit the wet silk and tormented me further.

"I think we've talked about this before. Who is in charge?"

"You Daddy, you. But please, I need you," I wheedled, hoping it would get me what I wanted.

My face fell when he chuckled and instead of doing as I bid, he got up and off the bed.

"What... where are you going?" I shouted after him as I sat up.

"You are a pushy boy and Daddy needs to remind you who's in charge," he shouted back over his shoulder before he disappeared.

My arse wriggled against the cover and my hands balled into fists, barely resisting the urge to stroke my cock. *Don't do it. You'll come before you get to the fun stuff.*

My eyes narrowed on Luke and I thanked the Lord when he came back into the room a mere few seconds later. Then the air got stuck in my lungs at the sight of him stood there, his arousal standing proud of his body. The purple head was smeared with pre-cum. My mouth dried at the thought of him letting me taste it.

The hand holding the paddle came into my line of vision and Luke gave me a feral smile that turned my insides to jelly. My cock throbbed with what was about to happen next.

"I want you to lie on your back with your head hanging off the end of the bed."

What?

My mouth opened and shut before I could form a question with all the visuals running wild in my mind. "How will you spank me that way, Daddy?" My brow wrinkled, then my blood turned molten at the expression that formed on his face.

"Oh don't you worry your pretty little head about that."

Seeing the devilish glint appear in his eyes, I wasn't sure I wanted to ask any more questions, so moved into the position he requested. Once my head was hanging off the end of the bed he stepped closer, his cock by my face. Suddenly it twigged what he might have in mind. My thighs clamped together and I sucked in several breaths, trying to hold back the urge to cum before he confirmed my suspicions.

His cock nudged at my lips and without thinking, I opened, greedy for a taste. I sucked him in, the position opening my throat and allowing him to sink a little deeper. Breathing through my nose, my taste buds were in heaven as Luke's unique flavour invaded my senses. The scent of his musk filled my nose as his balls touched my face while I sucked him as deep as my throat would allow.

Saliva dripped out of my mouth as my tongue pressed against the hard flesh, seeking more of Luke's flavour. His hips remained static letting me get used to the feel of him filling my mouth and my throat.

I brought my hands up to hold onto his thighs, letting him know I was okay, but instead of moving, he bent over me and lifted my legs off the mattress until my knees hit my shoulders. I'd never been more grateful for being on the skinny side as he bent me in half.

"Let go of my hips Baby, and hold your legs in this position."

At his husky demand, I found myself obeying, even when what was about to happen formed in my mind's eye. With my arse fully exposed, I clutched at my stockinged thighs. Folded in half this way, Luke's cock all but held me prisoner.

A shiver raced through me at the picture I made for Luke.

"If you want me to stop Baby, just release your legs okay," he rasped huskily.

I moved my head the fraction his cock allowed to show I understood, but there was no way I was letting go. I wanted this.

Chapter 16

Luke

The sight of Scott folded in half and holding his legs, displaying his pert arse covered in red silk, as his mouth sucked on my cock was something I didn't think I'd ever forget. The image was burning itself into my memory banks.

Fuck, he looks stunning.

As I inhaled the scent of cum and sweat, my gaze continued to roam hungrily over the vibrant red outfit he wore.

I'd nearly swallowed my tongue when he'd started to unbutton his shirt. The little minx loved to tease me, although this outfit was by far my favourite one. The red against his milky skin made him glow. The sheer stockings looked sexy with the tattoos around the tops of his thighs, now covered in lace. He made an alluring picture.

The feel of his lips clamping on my cock pulled me from my perusal and I met his heavy-lidded, begging eyes. Never one to deny him, I eased my pelvis back, giving him a chance to take a breath before I pushed back into the warm, wet heaven that was his mouth.

Scott had shown on several occasions he didn't mind his throat being filled with my cock and that he had great control over his gag reflex. So with that in mind, I thrust deep and held still as his cheeks hollowed. The suction caused my legs to wobble so I braced my bent knees against the bed. I rasped out a breath before pulling back, again giving him a chance to catch his breath before thrusting back in. All the blood in my body pooled in my groin as my cock was bathed in delicious heat that tried to take away all my self-control and kill all my brain cells.

My hand clenched around the paddle and I moved my gaze back to the arse that still held the plug. It was nestled perfectly between his cheeks and begged for me to spank it. A smile spread over my face as I leant over Scott's body using my knees to keep my balance. The mouth around my cock sucked harder, pulling me deeper as if Scott was readying himself for what was coming next.

Lifting the paddle I took a second to figure out the best angle, twisting the paddle in my hand until the padded side sat square over Scott's arse. I took a breath, trying to clear some of the pleasure clouding my mind. It didn't help with the increasing tingles creeping down my spine. Fuck, I wasn't going to last much longer.

Driven by that knowledge, I lifted my hand up then I brought the paddle down, hitting both cheeks squarely in the middle.

"Arggghhh," Scott groaned around my cock, before his lips clamped tight and his fingers whitened as he gripped his thighs. There was sweat sheening his face.

"That's it Baby," I rasped past the lust, my hand already lifting to deliver another blow, only this time I thrust my cock deeper into his throat. There was a gurgling and saliva spilt down the sides of Scott's face as his cheeks hollowed. His eyes gleamed up at me, encouraging me to do it again.

"You want more Baby?" His eyelids blinked rapidly and his hands clutched at his legs in answer.

With that, I let go. I gripped the paddled firmly and set a steady rhythm in time to the thrusts of my hips. The sound of Scott's choked mewls and the paddle hitting his flesh filled the room. As sweat dripped down my face, my breathing became choppy as I struggled to stop myself from coming before Scott.

His body strained and the spreading darkness on his silk panties spoke to how close he was. His lips clamped so tightly around my cock my hand faltered mid-air. Pleasure rocked through my body, and the tingling in my balls became almost painful as the first spurt of cum was released into his throat.

"Come Baby, come for Daddy," I cried out, blind to everything but the pleasure careening through me.

My body arched backwards, with my cock pulsing mercilessly as I was held captive by Scott's mouth. Desperately struggling to keep upright with spurt after spurt of cum filling his throat, I locked out my knees.

Scott's Adam's apple bobbed as he worked to swallow everything I gave him. His hips juddered and he gurgled loudly, forcing me to pull my cock free from his mouth. Sounds of raspy breaths and contented moans were his only response while his whole body shuddered in what appeared to be orgasmic bliss. With my legs continuing to judder under me, I gave up trying to remain standing and collapsed onto the carpet next to where Scott's head still hung off the bed.

When I blinked my eyes back into focus, I chuckled at Scott still holding onto his legs. The need to check he was okay fought past my exhaustion. "Baby, are you okay? You can let go of your legs."

His head turned towards me and a silly smile lit his face. A face that was covered in the remnants of his spit and my cum. "I think I'm stuck," he rasped through swollen lips.

Laughter rumbled through me at his ridiculousness. I dropped the paddle and held onto the bed to stand up on unsteady legs. Once I got my balance, I climbed on the mattress next to him. "Let me help. You might get pins and needles from holding this position for so long, so let's do one leg at a time." I took hold of the leg closest to me and rubbed at it as I lowered it to the bed. When he didn't complain, I did the other leg.

Once both were down, I tugged him into the centre of the bed, carefully lifting his head. "You can't be comfortable with your head hanging off the bed like that."

His drowsy gaze held mine. "It didn't seem to worry you earlier."

At the matter of fact way he spoke, I shrugged. There was really no answer to that, not when I'd make sure we did it again. He gave a sleepy chuckle and curled his body towards mine. "Aww fuck," he complained, his eyes flickering open as he stopped moving.

My heart rate, that had just started to return to normal, fired off like a rocket against my ribs.

"What? Did I hurt you? Oh my God it was too much—"

"Daddy, stop. Let me get a word in edgeways," he demanded, his voice full of exasperation. "No, it wasn't too much. It was amazing. I came so hard I thought I could see stars and you didn't even have to touch my cock." There was wonder on his face as he grinned at me. All the while his hand was gently stroking my arm. "My panties have glued themselves to me and they're trying to take off a layer of skin. That's what I'm complaining about."

The earnest expression said he was telling the truth. "Then let me help you get clean and then we can chill in bed." The smile he had on his face brightened so much it nearly blinded me. How was I going to cope when he went home on Tuesday?

My heart skipped a beat at the reality.

Don't think about it now.

As I got off the bed, I tucked the depressing thought away and helped Scott to the bathroom. Focusing all my attention on him, I took my time to wash him and dry him. By the time we returned to the bedroom, he could hardly keep his eyes open. We crawled into the bed and I settled back against the headboard as Scott lay against my chest. His breath teased my skin as he drifted off to sleep in my arms.

With nothing to distract me, my mind went back to the thoughts I'd dwelled on earlier. The loneliness I'd lived with for years had been a living, breathing thing inside me, yet Scott had somehow smothered it. The house only felt like a home when Scott was in it. Where does that leave me?

Over the last couple of days it had become apparent how much I wanted Scott in my life, more than the few hours we managed to juggle with work. The last few months, after this weekend, seemed to highlight how little time we actually had together. Was it too soon to talk about moving in together?

If I was honest with myself, it wasn't the first time I'd considered asking Scott that very question. What about his new job? Will that mean I'll see him even less? My hands trembled as I held Scott a little closer.

"You ok?" he mumbled, his eyes not opening as his arm slid over my waist.

"Shush now. Go back to sleep, Baby," I whispered, softly stroking his warm, naked back. He snuffled and whatever he said was lost as he buried his face in my neck.

I stared down at him and the confrontation Scott had had with Adam on Friday came back to me. I'd heard more than Scott's declaration of love. Adam's disbelief that we were still dating had been something I'd avoided thinking about. Why hadn't he admitted to Adam before Friday that we were still dating? *Didn't he confess to Adam that he loves you?* That was after Adam made him mad. *He introduced you to his family, did he not?*

Then why do I feel he's still holding back?

My mind drifted to Brett and the day before. I'd forgotten to tell him Scott was staying so he'd turned up for a chat.

The sound of the doorbell had Scott jerk in my lap. "Were you expecting anyone?" His brow wrinkled before he glanced towards the door leading to the hallway.

"Nope, but it will be Brett, he's the only one who would call on a Saturday, knowing I'm off. Shall we pretend we're not in," I asked hesitantly, not sure I was ready for the two most important people in my life to meet formally and maybe not like each other.

His answer was to wriggle off my lap.

"Okay then," I huffed, getting up and heading to the door as Scott stood, saying nothing.

In the hallway I took a breath and opened the door. "Hi, I wasn't expecting you this weekend."

His face was flushed with the cold as he shoved his hands into his jacket, avoiding looking me in the eye. "I figured if you didn't have anything on we could hang out."

As he finished, there was the sound of footsteps behind me and Scott appeared next to my arm.

"Oh... I didn't realise you had company. I'll leave you to it." Brett wagged his eyebrows at us with a forced exaggeration.

"Nah, come in. We've got leftover pizza and beer," Scott offered with a genuine smile on his face.

He gave me a nudge with his shoulder and the love that was becoming my constant companion filled me with warmth. "There's your answer," I said, glancing back at Brett with a smile splitting my face.

Scott's mouth moved against my flesh and goosebumps sprang to life and reminded me of where I was and how fucking lucky I was. The afternoon we'd spent lazing around eating pizza and drinking beer had been fun and, as it turned out, Brett and Scott got on like a house on fire.

Without the worries that the two most important people in my life wouldn't get on, the question came back. Was it too early to ask Scott to move in?

I shut my eyes and prayed that if I slept on it, I would find the answer, and soon.

Chapter 17

Scott

Music pumped out of hidden speakers as I lay my head against the large sofa cushion when it refused to hold itself up. I grinned stupidly at Adam and Richie as they swayed drunkenly around Lenny and Nathan's apartment. The city lights sparkled against the glass in the background since Lenny had dimmed the lights. Candles flickered around the room, casting shadows that danced over the wall and gave the room a romantic feel.

With the abundance of pink flamingo motifs over everything, it kind of made it all a little vulgar. Nothing appeared to escape the pink bird, from the stuffed animals, bean bags, plates and glasses all scattered around the room. Hell, even Ferron had managed to find a shirt with flamingos on. It had caused quite a stir when he'd said he'd had it in the back of his wardrobe. I mean who has a shirt with pink flamingos on?

Ferron.

As I giggled, Bailey, who was sat next to me, lifted his head and glanced in my direction. "What you laughin' at?" he slurred, his eyes squinting at me before they looked about the room. As his gaze came back to mine, Bailey burst out laughing. "Forget I asked that," he said through the laughter.

With my curiosity piqued, I glanced back at the room and my mouth dropped open. Ferron lay on one of the bean bags, clutching one of the giant stuffed flamingos. He was covered in a brown substance. A vague memory floated into my mind, past the haze of alcohol, of Adam betting Ferron he couldn't drink from the chocolate fountain while riding the stuffed flamingo.

The hilarity it caused had been a welcome relief after I'd thought I'd be spending a night alone again, because Luke had a work function to oversee. When Lenny had rung me this afternoon, asking if I was up to coming to his for drinks and food, it had been a no brainer.

When Adam and Carl had only given everyone four weeks' notice of their Valentine's wedding, it had created a state of panic. Lenny had mentioned Nathan's moaning about how inconsiderate they were to land him with the best man duties when he had so much on his plate. I chuckled recalling Adam telling Lenny about how Carl had sent him to ensure Nathan agreed to be his best man. Adam, I knew, had a look that rivalled mine and could get people to do exactly what he wanted.

It seemed Isaac, though, wasn't happy with Nathan's lack of effort in regards to a stag do, so had sorted it himself instead, arranging a day of activities for the Doms. Not that he'd told Lenny what they were before he'd whisked Nathan away, much to Lenny's displeasure.

Nathan's old army sergeant, Bailey, who was visiting and also a sub, wasn't invited either so had the brilliant idea that Lenny should host a stag party for Adam. So here we were, several hours later, a little worse for wear and, it would appear, some of us caked in chocolate.

"Anyone want another drink?" Lenny shouted over the music and I struggled to lift my head to look over at him, slumped on the other huge sofa. Gauging from his slurred words, I figured he wasn't fairing much better than the rest of us.

I eyed the table in front of me and the half-consumed cocktail Adam had made for me and shook my head, though I wasn't sure if he even noticed when his eyelids drooped closed.

Adam staggered against Richie, but whatever he said was drowned out by the music.

Richie giggled and tugged Adam closer. My gaze roamed the room.

Where had Sawyer gone?

Heat spread up my neck at the game of truth or dare we'd played earlier. I fanned my face and shifted on the cushion. Having been in the doll drums since I'd left Luke's home on Tuesday morning, my friends were exactly what I'd needed.

The only problem was, it reminded me that I'd been avoiding mentioning to Luke about the wedding invitation Adam had given me. Even with Adam poking at me about who I was bringing to the wedding as my plus one, I'd not mentioned it to Luke.

I chewed my lower lip in between my teeth. The alcohol that was swimming through my veins didn't hide the tension that formed at the base of my neck. *Just ask him to come with you.*

Once my brain latched onto the idea, in my drunken state it wouldn't let go. I squinted at my wristwatch. Would Luke be finished work now? *Of course he would be, it's one in the morning you idiot.*

"I'm not an idiot," I mumbled as I staggered to my feet.

"Who's not an idiot?" Bailey slurred, right before he tilted sideways and landed on the sofa, his face mushed into the cushion, appearing out for the count.

I waved at the room in general as I swayed to the door, rooting in my pocket for my phone to open the app to get an Uber. Hoping I'd typed in the address right, I stepped into the hall. I eyed the lift and sniffed. The stairs being the only option, I started to regret them by the time I'd walked down four flights. Hanging onto the railing, I glanced down then wished I hadn't when a wave of dizziness hit me. With my stomach trying to rebel, I prayed I'd not be sick as I inhaled and exhaled twice before I could manage the remaining steps.

Outside, the icy air blasted through my shirt and I glanced down, realising I'd left my jacket in Lenny's apartment.

"Fuck shi—" I jerked back from the curb when I car pulled to halt in front of me and any thought I might have had about retrieving my jacket fled with the need to get out of the cold. I opened the door and hoped I looked sensible enough.

"Scott?" The guy asked, without even glancing back at me.

"Yeah," I answered, before sliding into the warm confines of the car. I shivered and goosebumps spread all over my body.

As the driver took off, I was catapulted back into the seat, cursing under my breath when my clumsy fingers couldn't get the clasp to slot into the buckle. I grappled with the seat belt and eventually managed to get the fastener into the slot, then slumped back in the seat.

I scratched at my chin. Maybe I should go home? *Luke is home.*

A silly grin spread over my face at my answer.

Ever since Luke had dropped me home at the beginning of the week, I'd felt unsettled, like there was a piece missing and I couldn't locate it. *Luke's what's missing, so stop kidding yourself it's anything else.*

The drunken voice in my head caused me to chuckle at having all the answers I needed.

I glanced out the window at the passing lights whizzing by and tried to figure out how long it would be before I got to Luke's. After a few seconds I gave up when all it did was make my head ache and made me feel a little dizzy. I shut my eyes and rested my head back against the seat.

"Hoy mate, we 'ere," came a voice that I didn't recognise, as I roused myself.

I blinked my eyes, then rubbed at them until I could focus. Shit, I'd fallen asleep in the back of the Uber. I shifted onto my hip, still feeling groggy as I rooted through my pocket to pay.

"You've already paid with your card mate," the guy stated, his impatient gaze meeting mine.

"Sorry," I mumbled and let out a relieved breath when the seatbelt behaved itself and released first time.

Once I got out of the car, and it drove off, I noticed Luke's home was in darkness. *Bugger, now what?*

Without the security lights, I struggled to make out if his car was parked on the drive. I took a couple of steps closer to the house and was suddenly blinded by the bright lights that came on. As my eyes watered, I ran up the path and before I could think about it, I knocked hard on the door. Through watery eyes, I glanced at the well-lit drive and Luke's car.

Yay, he's here.

After what felt like forever, but was probably only a couple of minutes, the door opened. I offered a big grin. "Helllllloooo Daddyyyyy."

"What... what on earth Scott? Are you drunk?"

I met his gaze, my brows pinched and the smile fell from my lips. Was he pissed off with me for coming to see him?

"I came to see if you wanted to come to Adam's wedding with me," I explained, not sure at all why we were having this conversation on the doorstep.

"Dear Lord, what am I going to do with you," he muttered, and then sighed as he took hold of my arm and guided me inside.

With the door shutting out the chill, it was only then I noticed I was shaking and my teeth felt like they were rattling in my mouth. *Where's my jacket?*

"What's up Daddyyy," I slurred as he took a firmer hold of me when I swayed on the spot.

"When you're sober, I'll answer that question, Baby. But right now, I need to get you warmed up and several glasses of water inside you so you won't feel like death warmed up in the morning."

"I'm just tipsssyyy, that's all." I grinned up at him, hoping he'd see I was okay.

He shook his head and guided me up to his bedroom. Once there I tried and failed several times to unbutton my shirt. My hands were knocked out of the way. "Hey, I do it."

"Is Luke deaf?"

"No Luke is not deaf, but you are clearly drunk," he ground out, sounding more than a little pissed off.

"Had I said that aloud?"

"Yes, you did," he answered as his mouth appeared to twitch.

"Wow Daddy, you're reading my mind. I knew we had a connection but this is—"

"God love me and save me," he muttered before I had a chance to finish talking. With all my energy seeming to have left me, I couldn't find the strength to argue as I was tucked into the big, warm bed.

Luke fussed for a few seconds, making sure I was wrapped in the brushed, cotton duvet. "I'll be back in a minute with some water." As Luke spoke he went to the far side of the room and retrieved the bin that was sat by the dressing table. He placed it next to the side of the bed. "If you want to be sick, all you need to do is roll over, okay?"

There were deep grooves around Luke's mouth by the time he finished talking, but the warmth of the bed made it difficult for me to form a sentence, so I nodded. Or I thought I did, but I couldn't be sure.

"What am I going to do with you?"

"Keep me," I whispered into the pillow.

Chapter 18

Luke

"Will you tell me what on earth is wrong? Because, if you don't I'm going to quit. You've been like a bear with a sore head since you came into work on Monday," Sarah demanded. Her hands were on her hips and her chin was thrust forward. Her eyes were firing all sorts of warnings at me.

I rubbed at my face, feeling the six o'clock shadow. What was wrong with me?

As if you don't know.

Ever since I'd opened the door to find a very drunk Scott on my doorstep after a shit evening at work, I hadn't known what to do with myself. The feelings of elation at him just showing up left me in no doubt that I wanted him in my home and in my life on a permanent basis. His drunken announcement that he wanted me to attend Carl and Adam's wedding as his partner even took away all the worry I had that he wasn't ready to show those closest to him, what I meant to him.

Then, hard on its heels, were his whispered words. "Keep me." They continued to play over and over in my head like a broken record. I'd somehow developed an ache in my chest that only Scott's presence could fix.

The question of me asking him if he wanted to move in with me, nagged to the point I was struggling to think about anything else. It was like a blood-sucking tick that had burrowed into my skin. It wasn't for letting go without a fight.

"Hello, earth to Luke, come in Luke, Sarah is about ready to blow a gasket," Sarah said, super sweetly. Although there was nothing sweet about her expression, forcing me to give an apologetic smile, knowing fine well I'd zoned out on her again.

"I'm sorry… what were we talking about?"

"Jesus. You're having a laugh with me right?" The exasperation in her voice was matched by the arched brows that, a second later, disappeared under her fringe.

Oh, that was not good.

Her hand came up as she stepped up to the desk, and leant over it. Her red pointy fingernail nearly drilled a hole in my chest, though I didn't move with her steely gaze pinning me in place.

"Now you listen to me and you listen well. Go home, fix whatever has you behaving this way and make sure that when you return tomorrow, you bring in a new and improved version. One that won't find himself looking for a new personal assistant, got it?"

My mouth opened, a denial on the tip of my tongue.

"Forget it. You will not give me any bullshit nonsense about everything being fine, because it's clearly not."

This time, I could hear genuine concern in her voice, so I swallowed back the lie and nodded. "Okay, I'll go because you're right. I do need to pull my head out of my arse. If I carry on this way, it won't be you out of a job, but me. Griffin won't tolerate me not delivering on the tight schedule we have for the refurbishments."

She rolled her eyes at me. "He'll never sack you. You work far too hard..." This time I rolled my eyes at her. "Alright, you normally work very hard. This is just a blip... can I ask, is everything alright with you and Scott?"

"As it seems you've already asked me, I'll answer you. We're fine. Hell, we're more than fine. It's just... that I've got something on my mind and I don't know what to do about it," I finished lamely, doing my best not to meet her gaze.

"You can talk to me? Or why not speak to Brett? He's good at talking things through with you, is he not?" When my ex, Brody, had shown up with Nick, his new partner, to confront me last year, I'd been a mess afterwards and Sarah had called Brett because she'd not known what to do with a blubbering boss. He'd come to the rescue and received Sarah's undying devotion.

"I'll give him a ring and see if he's free."

With that, I got up and eyed my overflowing desk.

"I'll work through what I can. Go." Her hands ushered me towards the door.

"Alright, I'm going," I complained without heat. I grabbed my coat and left before I could change my mind. Checking my phone as I got to the lift, I scrolled through my contacts to find Brett's work number. He never had his mobile on at work, explaining that his office was a mobile phone-free space. That if his clients weren't allowed to bring their phones into his office, then neither should he.

When his secretary put me straight through to him, I saw it as a sign. "Hi, are you free to meet up?"

"Give me a sec," he asked as the sound of paper rustling came through the speaker. "I've got about an hour and a half before my next appointment. It might be best though if you come here and we can head to the coffee shop in the lobby. I've got some notes I need to write up," he explained distractedly.

"Fine, I'll see you in a bit," I answered, but the sound of the dial tone was my only response. Used to Brett when his mind was occupied with clients, I didn't get offended. Putting my phone into my suit jacket pocket, I exited the lift and walked through the hotel lobby. It was only when I'd made it outside without having to stop and talk to someone that I released the breath I'd been holding.

In the car, I cursed and tried to recall if there had been any news bulletins about new road works as I got stuck in gridlocked traffic. By the time I got to Brett's office, I barely had thirty minutes left of the time he'd had available. As I entered the lobby of the building, I saw him waving at me from the coffee shop window.

There were sandwiches sat with two jumbo-sized coffees that took the edge off my sizzling temper. "I really hate London sometimes." I growled loudly as I plonked myself down in the empty seat and ignored the lady at the next table who gave me a sharp look.

"What's new?" Brett stated as he gave me a big grin and picked up his half-eaten sandwich.

Not sure if he was answering my comment or asking because of my request to meet, I went with the latter. "Is it too soon to ask Scott to move in with me?"

Brett coughed and spluttered. The half-chewed Tuna and mayo on the brown bread he'd been eating, sprayed the table, forcing me to sit back. "Hey, you're supposed to eat that, not spray me with it."

His eyes narrowed as he struggled to swallow, while picking up a napkin to wipe at his hand. After he'd cleaned up, he dropped the napkin and picked up his coffee, taking two big sips. Only when the cup was back on the table did he answer me. "Why are you asking me? Only you have the answer, Luke. How many times have we talked about Scott since I came to your place last weekend?" His brows rose as he waited for me to answer.

"I don't know… a few?" Heat crept up my face at his sardonic expression said I knew fine well how many times we'd talked. "Okay, a lot. What does that have to do with anything?"

He leant closer and took hold of the hand I was using to play with the wrapping on my sandwich, stopping me from fidgeting. "When you were with Brody, how often did you talk about your relationship with me?"

His hand tightened on mine as I went to move it. "Not often, but then there was never much to say until it was over."

"Exactly, when it was over—"

"What the hell does that mean?" I demanded, my frustration not abating as I'd hoped.

"You talk about Scott all the time. In fact, he's all you ever talk about now. You light up when he's mentioned. You're excited in ways I've never seen you before. Brody, no in fact *all* the men you've dated, never lit a spark in you. There was always this need to fight for domination between you and whoever was the flavour of the month, because you denied a fundamental part of yourself.

"With Scott you don't have to do that. The side of you that wants to nurture and look after Scott, be the 'Daddy', has been freed. The way you are with him is lovely to see. I've honestly never seen you happier than when you are with him." His hand held mine for another moment, before he released me.

But I was too shocked to do more than stare at him open-mouthed as the truth behind the words struck home. Oh, I'd known that there was something lacking from my past relationships, I'd just never considered I'd been that unhappy in them. Not until Brett pointed it out.

Scott was the light of my life. No matter how hard I tried, I couldn't imagine a life without him in it. *Then why haven't you asked him to move in with you?*

"I'm holding myself back, aren't I?" Even as the question popped out, I didn't need Brett to answer.

"You've hidden for so long that it's hard to take a step, knowing that the other person has the power to crush your heart." As he spoke, his eyes clouded over but before I could say anything, his phone rang.

He lifted it and sighed. "I'm sorry but my next appointment has arrived early. I'm going to have to go." He stood and hesitated. "Are the feelings you have for Scott worth the leap of faith? If the answer is yes, then you have your answer."

He bent and brushed his lips against my cheek. "He loves you and you love him, cherish it for what it is," he whispered into my ear, before he stood and gave me a quick wave then strode off without a backwards glance.

I sat and watched as he stiffly walked away until he disappeared from view.

Had he loved Nigel like I love Scott?

With no answer, tension gathered at the base of my skull and I squeezed at my neck. Brett's parting words continued to play on my mind as I stared at the crowded lobby, my coffee going cold. After a few minutes, I got up and left the untouched food and walked outside. With no real destination in mind, I strolled down the streets that were teeming with people who bustled past me.

I paid no mind to the grey sky and chilly wind that tugged at my jacket as my pace slowed and I realised I was outside La Trattoria Di Amore. The glass doors gleamed and seemed to invite a person to stop and go in. The door opened and two men exited, bringing with them the scent of sumptuous Italian food. My stomach gurgled and reminded me I hadn't eaten.

One of the men held the door open and his dark brow rose.

Before I knew what I was doing, I'd stepped inside.

Adam's head lifted from whatever he was looking at, the welcoming smile dimming slightly when he saw me. "Luke." He nodded curtly at me.

I glanced towards the partition separating the foyer from the main restaurant then I shifted my gaze back to Adam. My fingernails dug into my palms. "I love him. I know I've been a shit in the past, but I love Scott more than you'll ever know. Nothing is going to change that and I want you to know I won't hurt him." I blurted out, not sure who was more shocked, him or me.

Judging by the way his lips were flapping open and shut, I'd say it was a close call.

"Well… okay… I'm not quite sure what to say to that." He held up his hands before they flopped back down to his sides.

"Scott asked me to come as his plus one to your wedding, is that okay? If me being there spoils your day, then I'll come up with an excuse." It pained me to say it, but I knew it was the right thing to do.

Adam's eyes narrowed on me and he stared at me for what felt like long minutes before he finally spoke. "When Scott told me you were coming, he could hardly sit still he was so excited. I might still have some reservations, but I can see that you do love him. So if Scott believes that you've changed then I can accept that you have."

About to step forward and offer my hand I froze.

"But if you so much as cause him to regret falling in love with you, I'll get my soon to be husband to kick your arse, agreed?" he growled, his face fierce.

I nodded and then lifted my hand. "Agreed."

"Adam can I hav—" Scott appeared and pulled up short as he eyed both Adam and I. The smile on his face disappeared as his hands went to his hips. "What's going on here?"

On hearing the edge of panic in his voice, I released Adam's hand and closed the gap to Scott. As I took hold of his arms, I kissed his pouty lips. "Hey Baby. I came to see when you were going to be finished. I have the afternoon off and I wanted to spend some time with my man." Scott's face got a dreamy expression as I wrapped my arms around him.

"I've another half an hour before I can escape. Will you wait for me?" He glanced at Adam then back at me, chewing his lip.

"I'll sit out here and wait. Adam will keep me entertained, I'm sure," I joked and let out a quiet sigh of relief when he nodded and grinned at Scott.

Chapter 19

Scott

I raced back into the dining room and tried to keep Seb from noticing how I encouraged the few straggler diners to hurry up and leave. The lunch service had been madly busy and I'd not had five minutes to myself.

With the hope I could maybe cut out early whirling around my mind, I went to the bar to continue helping set up the empty tables.

I eyed Theo thoughtfully. Would he cover for me?

"What's put a rocket up your backside," Theo whispered as we stood at the bar collecting clean glasses.

"Luke's here," I whispered back, unable to stop the big grin spreading over my face.

"Were you expecting him?" Theo asked quietly, his brows rising before he darted a quick look over his shoulder.

"Nah, he just showed up."

"You want me to cover your tables? You've done it often enough for me." Theo gave me a nudge in Seb's direction. "Go ask Seb can you go early. I'm sure he'll say yes."

With the urge to fist pump the air at Theo's offer, I glanced at Seb, trying to gauge what mood he was in. Seeing as he was smiling and looking relaxed, I nodded at Theo, then walked over to where Seb was standing. Resisting the urge to slump and shove my hands into my too-tight trouser pockets, I gave Seb my most winning smile.

"Do you want something Scott?" His eyes lit with amusement as he spoke.

"Erm... you see... Luke is here and I wondered if I could leave a little early. Theo said he'd cover my tables," I rushed to explain.

Seb glanced between Theo and me before he nodded. "That's fine. Off you go."

Not giving him a chance to say anything else, I kept to a dignified pace as I hightailed it into the kitchen. Going straight to the locker room, I changed into my clothes and was back in the entrance of the restaurant in a matter of minutes, only wheezing slightly.

The smile on Luke's face when I appeared didn't help my breathlessness. He stood and held out his hand, taking hold of my rucksack. "Come on, let's go." His hazel eyes held my attention when they glowed with something that made my heart dance in my chest.

"See you at the wedding," Adam called out as we walked to the door.

I stopped and glanced back, heat riding up my face. Luke hadn't given me an answer as yet and I wasn't sure what to say.

"That you will," Luke answered, taking away my dilemma and leaving me dumbstruck.

Outside, he took hold of my hand and directed me down the street. My mind reeled at his response to Adam. Had Adam mentioned the wedding to guilt Luke into coming with me?

Why would you think that?

Luke loves me, so why wouldn't he want to come with me?

With the questions going around in circles and Luke making no effort to hold a conversation, I tried to focus on an unexpected afternoon together.

As we continued to stroll into London city centre, there was a companionable silence between us that neither of us seemed inclined to break.

With the busy lunch rush and no break, after thirty minutes my legs were starting to feel weary. About to ask why we were still walking, I noticed where we were. "Did you come to meet Brett for lunch?"

Luke's stride faltered for a moment and his fingers tightened around mine. A sense of unease settled in the pit of my stomach when his jaw bunched. When no answer was forthcoming, I pushed. "Is that why you weren't parked at the restaurant?" I'd thought it a little odd when he'd gone past the car park back at the restaurant. Then I'd put it down to it maybe being full as the restaurant had been fully booked.

"Yes, I needed to have a chat with him."

Luke's response was too vague to gauge what the talk might have been about, and his eyes were staring straight ahead. Was I missing something? It sure as hell felt like it.

We crossed a street and Luke guided me towards the NCP car park. Once we got to the car, I got in and fidgeted in the seat. An increasing sense of panic took hold when Luke got in the car and acted like I wasn't there.

As I scratched at my ear, then tugged on the ends of my hair, Luke pulled out into the traffic, concentrating on the road. My head was pounding by the time we were nearly at Luke's home. I bit at my lower lip, stopping myself from demanding what was wrong while he was driving.

All the euphoria I'd felt at seeing Luke had long since disappeared by the time he pulled into his driveway, having remained stoically silent throughout the drive. I all but jumped out of the car, spoiling for a fight. His face was a neutral mask as he got out of the car, seemingly unaware of how his behaviour was affecting me.

As he made his way up the path, my teeth gritted together and my hands balled at my sides. I stomped past him, convinced I had steam coming out of my ears as he opened the door to let me into the house. Inside the hallway, I heard the door shut behind me and I whisked around to face Luke. My mouth gaped open when he spoke.

"Will you move in with me?" His voice sounded like he'd swallowed glass, and his eyes conveyed a depth of emotion that poleaxed me. Did he just ask me to move in with him? Was this why he'd been acting funny? Why didn't he just ask me in the car?

Seeing his face become closed off, something I hadn't experienced since our first date, and not something I ever wanted to see again, I launched myself at him. Climbing up him like a monkey would a tree, I firmly pushed the questions buzzing around my head aside. "Daddy, don't you dare pull a stunt like that again," I reprimanded as I kissed his stiff lips, my legs locking around his waist as my arms wrapped around his neck. "You had me all worried in the car with the silent treatment." I continued to explain, punctuating each word with a kiss to his face. A feeling of relief filled me as his hands cupped my backside and held on to me. "You're so naughty making me worry like that—"

"Are you going to answer my question?" he growled as his groin was pressed firmly against mine. All the blood circulating in my head decided to travel south, making it nigh on impossible to concentrate on anything other than the throbbing occurring in my pants.

Luke's mouth hovered over mine and his tongue swept along my lips. "Answer me, Baby." The husky demand got my head nodding as I chased his lips when he shifted his head back.

"Daddy, stop teasing meeee," I whined and wriggled against him.

"Then answer my question, I need to hear you say it."

The seriousness in his voice penetrated past my lust and I sucked in a breath and met his gaze. There was so much love shining out at me, I didn't know how there was any left in the world for anyone else. How was this beautiful man mine?

It only matters that he is.

Unhooking my arms from around his neck, I took hold of his face. "I love you and you're never going to get rid of me now. Once I move in, you'll need more than dynamite to shift me. So be sure that's what you want, Daddy."

The air got stuck in my chest as his eyes gleamed with affection and he moved to rub the tip of his nose against mine. "You're ridiculous, you know that?" he said, his voice full of affection.

"Yes, but I'm your ridiculous Baby, and that's what counts," I whispered.

"You are and have been since I followed you into the lift all those months ago. I didn't know there was more to life, to love, until you. You will forever be my always more," he breathed out and his hot breath brushed at my lips. About to move to kiss him, I was stopped by the look in his eyes.

"So are we going to be spending the afternoon packing up your things?" There was an edge of uncertainty to his voice that hadn't been there seconds earlier.

"Well, we could"—I ground my lower body against his and fluttered my eyelashes—"or we could go upstairs and I could unpack the clothes I'm wearing." I rubbed my nose against his as a suggestive smile spread over my face. "That would make more sense, especially as Daddy might like to help with the unpacking." I arched my brows before I shifted my gaze to my groin.

A light dawned on Luke's face as he followed my gaze. One of the hands cupping my arse moved up to the waistband of my jeans. "Is that right?" His lips pursed before a moan left his mouth. "I think my Baby's right," he finished breathlessly, as his fingers touched the lacy band of my underwear.

"Good answer Daddy, good answer."

Epilogue

LUKE

Subtle music played in the background and didn't prevent me from hearing the conversations flowing around me as I searched for Scott. He'd left me to go and organise the wait staff two hours earlier and I'd only caught brief glimpses of him since then.

There was a large crowd spread around The Flamingo Bar and waiters, in their distinctive uniform of fitted black trousers, stark white shirts and bright pink dickie bows with white flamingos on, roamed with trays laden with champagne.

Scott, as the head waiter, wore a black shirt instead of the white, and his dickie bow was white with pink flamingos. With a quick glance at those standing close to me, I moved my jacket to hide my body's reaction to the image that had formed in my mind of Scott wearing the dickie bow and the white and pink lacy bodysuit I'd found to match.

The moment I'd seen the bowtie I hadn't been able to resist searching for something he could wear under his work clothes just for my pleasure.

There was a nudge to my elbow from behind and I glanced back at the dark, bearded guy trying to place him. Given a guided tour by Scott when I'd arrived, I was sure he'd introduced me to this guy. My gaze narrowed… Boyd.

If I was right, this was the guy who'd done the renovations and building work, though he looked nothing like a builder dressed in a beautifully cut, dove grey suit, with a dark grey shirt and tie. I offered the hand not holding a glass of champagne and smiled. "I have to congratulate you Boyd. The workmanship is fantastic. I wasn't sure what to expect, but the beautiful handcrafted bar, booths and tables show original workmanship. You've created a sophisticated feel to the place. I love it." I glanced around the room before looking back at him, "I'm going to enjoy coming here with Scott."

His face was a myriad of emotions, none of which were there long enough for me to gauge what he was thinking. "I'm just grateful we managed to complete it on time and that it turned out okay."

There was none of the joy I'd have expected to hear in his voice, so I shrugged and glanced away. Unsure what to say to break the tension that seemed to mount with each passing second, I remained silent.

"There you are, I've been looking for you," came a soft voice I recognised.

About to answer, my lips clamped together when I realised he wasn't talking to me. There was an awkward moment when I glanced between Sawyer, Scott's friend and work colleague, and Boyd. Sawyer had eyes for only one man, his gaze firmly fixed on Boyd and his answering smile. *Scott never mentioned Sawyer and Boyd were an item?*

Since Scott had moved in with me two months earlier, I'd encouraged him to invite his friends over, particularly when he had a night off and I was working. He hated when I wasn't there and vice versa, but with our jobs not being nine-to-five, Monday to Friday, we'd had to adjust. *Would you go back to being alone?* Hell, no.

Life with Scott was... life-affirming. There was no other way to put it. He was everything and more. I'd never been so happy and the little box that was hidden at home was a testament to how serious I was about him. I'd taken Brett with me only two weeks earlier, when Scott was at work, to buy a ring. Now all I needed was the right moment.

All the moments are the right ones.

The distinct sounding voice of Brett was ignored. He'd already asked me four times why I hadn't proposed yet. With very little time together over the last few weeks, with Scott busy helping to get The Flamingo Bar ready for tonight's grand opening, there hadn't been a moment that felt right. A part of me figured I'd know when it was, so I tried not to stress about it.

"—isn't that right Luke?" Sawyer asked, his face full of expectation.

Oh shit. *What had he said?*

The feel of heat spreading up my neck caused me to offer an apologetic smile. "I'm sorry, I was admiring the décor. What did you say?"

"I said, doesn't the place look fantastic? Boyd's handcrafted bar is so beautiful and the fact it's all reclaimed wood really speaks to his dedication to protecting the planet," he gushed, while Boyd's face turned a rather alarming shade of red. "And after all the cr—"

"Luke doesn't need to know about that, Sawyer," Boyd said, interrupting Sawyer. His caramel eyes spoke volumes, throwing out a clear "shut up" that Sawyer looked about to argue with. Then Boyd moved and whispered something in Sawyer's ear and his face brightened. There was something that passed between them that made me feel like I was intruding.

Was I supposed to ignore what Sawyer was talking about?

Feeling at a loss, I searched the room for Scott, again. Seeing him at the bar, I gave the two men a smile. "I'm just going to see if I can speak to Scott for a moment." I breathed a sigh of relief when neither man seemed inclined to encourage me to linger.

Stopped several times by people I knew through the hotel, by the time I made it to where I'd seen Scott, he'd disappeared again. I rested my arm on the bar and huffed in frustration.

"How are you Luke? Are you enjoying the evening?" Seb asked, his voice holding just a hint of steel as I jerked and turned to his meet his hard stare.

"Good evening, Seb." I waved my hand towards the full room. "You must be pleased with the turnout. Scott advises the restaurant is already booked solid for the next three months."

"It is and we are. Carl is extremely pleased we could combine his two ventures." He wore a neutral expression but I got the distinct impression there was an underlying hostility just beneath the surface.

"Is there a problem Seb? I'm getting a feeling there is." My brows rose as I eyed him with trepidation. The memory of how Scott had found out about the dead animal pushed to the surface. Was my past going to keep biting me in the arse?

"There will be no problem as long as you take care of your... boy." The pause before he used a term only a Daddy would understand ensured he had my full attention.

"You're not threatening me?" I ground out through my clenched jaw as I stepped closer to him.

His hand came up as he looked unconcerned by my show of aggression. "You can take it any way you want. I've known Scott for many years and he is precious and can be easily damaged by someone who doesn't understand him."

Affronted by Seb's tone and the implied inference I would hurt Scott, my fingernails bit into the flesh of my palms. *Its Scott's boss, don't lamp him one, not tonight.*

Inhaling deeply, I exhaled and willed myself to keep hold of the temper sizzling inside my veins. "I love Scott. He is my life." My heart trembled in my chest at the truth behind the words. "There is nothing I wouldn't do for him, to keep him safe, or to protect him. So you can stop with your threats, they're pointless."

Seb's face relaxed and a smile tugged at the corners of his mouth. "I needed to be sure about how you feel about him. I can clearly see I don't need to worry," he explained, as if that automatically made everything alright.

Not feeling at all appeased, I struggled to not go with my first instinct and punch him in the face to wipe off the smug look he was now sporting.

Movement and a dark head caught my attention and I let out a relieved sigh when Scott walked towards us through the crowd. His face was alight with happiness as he stopped in front of me and offered up his mouth. The anger melted away as I bent and gave him what he wanted. I gently brushed my mouth against his, tasting something sweet.

"Have you been at the desserts already?" I chuckled when he flushed and licked at his mouth, before he glanced at Seb looking decidedly guilty.

"I might have had to have a small taste. You know, to check they were okay for the party-goers." His eyelashes fluttered at Seb, who laughed.

"Stop with the eyes, for Christ's sake." Seb glanced in my direction, asking, "How on earth do you stop yourself from caving in with that look?" His face was full of sympathy as he glanced between the two of us. Before I could answer, a voice came from behind Seb.

"The same way I would think you deal with it… Daddy," Richie joked, as he gave Seb an almost identical look to the one Scott had given me.

I roared with laughter when Seb flushed and his eyes narrowed on Richie, but I'd not missed the adoration in his expression.

"Come here troublemaker," Seb demanded as humour danced on his face.

Richie went into Seb's open arms willingly, a breathtaking smile lighting his expression as he tucked his head into Seb's shoulder. "Yes, Daddy."

All Seb did was roll his eyes at me and Scott, who'd moved to stand next to me.

As I wrapped my arm around Scott's back and glanced down at him, my heart stuttered. The noise, the people around us, disappeared as the love shining up at me gave me hope that there would indeed be always more with my man.

What more could a person wish for?

This is the end for Luke and Scott but you'll find more of them in some of my other books. If you want to try a sample of one of my other books Christmas Beyond Christmas read on:

Prologue

Greg

2007

The pain in my legs increased as they were pushed unceremoniously into the locker, the jeering getting louder.

"It's too fucking funny man, how tiny you are," Ray mocked.

"Come on, get him in before anyone catches us," Billy said, a hint of apprehension in his voice as he held onto my ankles while trying to use his free hand to push my head in the locker.

The other three guys laughed as they finally managed to squish me into the small space meant for my books. The metal edges dug into my hips, my head hitting the back with a thud as the door was slammed shut and darkness descended. I blinked and tried to get a little more comfortable, not knowing how long I'd be in there.

I'd long since passed the point of trying to fight, because what was the point? They'd still win. I'd still find myself in the locker, only with a lot more bruises.

If you'd been paying attention instead of having your nose stuck in a book, you might have noticed Ray and his gang of dumbasses.

My brother's voice in my head overrode my thoughts and I sighed because he was right. I tended not to notice what was going on around me once I was lost in the pages of a book. They made a shitty school life better. In fact, they were the only thing that helped me survive the torment of being the smallest boy in school. It didn't help that I had blond curls and blue eyes with long eyelashes that the girls always complained weren't fair for a boy to have. And the boys just thought I looked gay. I'd discovered over the last year that they weren't wrong, my body starting to take notice of... Will.

Heat suffused my face and I squirmed in discomfort at the thought of the huge giant who was my older brother's best friend. The guy was a mountain. He'd started to grow rapidly at the age of twelve and hadn't stopped since. Now, at eighteen, he was the biggest guy in school, as broad as he was tall. No one messed with him. He was five years my senior and I worshipped him, not that he knew that.

As if I'd conjured him up, a deep voice I'd have recognized anywhere shouted something outside the locker, the door wrenched open a second later. I blinked owlishly at him as the light blinded me.

"Why is it that the minute I turn my back, you find yourself in trouble, Tiny?" His large hands took hold of me as he carefully lifted me out of the locker and placed me on the floor. His hands lingered on my waist as I found my footing.

My neck craned backwards so I could look up at his face. There was a familiar glint of anger simmering in the sea-green eyes. "I'm a magnet that shitty people stick to, what can I say?" I muttered, doing my best to keep the heat creeping up my neck from climbing any higher as Will took it upon himself to dust me off.

No matter how many times I told myself Will was just acting like one of my brothers, my heart didn't listen as it leapt with joy at his actions.

"If you took your head out of those damn books for a second, you might notice what's going on around you," he growled as he stood to his full height, towering over me.

His brows drew together and I braced myself for the lecture that was coming my way.

"I've told you before, you need to learn some self-defense. That way you can stop those dicks from hurting you. You have to stand up to the bullies. Neither me nor Neil will be here next semester to stop this shit from happening."

The genuine concern in his voice continued to play havoc with my heart as it swelled with teenage love and gratitude. It wasn't the first time that either him or Neil, my brother, had offered to teach me some basic moves. The problem was, I was about as coordinated as a piece of cooked spaghetti, which moved in any direction but the one I wanted it to. I didn't need to humiliate myself further by failing and having them witness it.

His broad shoulders stiffened as he stared at me as if he could read my mind.

"There's no point, Will. Whatever you teach me won't be enough to defend myself from Ray and his dick friends. Besides, they'll only be here for another year and then they'll be gone the same as you and Neil." The sadness in my voice caused the furrows on his forehead to deepen.

I forced a smile as I patted his bulging forearm. "Don't worry, I'll be fine."

His brows arched up in disbelief as he looked at the locker I'd been crammed into only minutes before. "Yeah Tiny, like that's true." He turned his head, his eyes narrowing as he scanned the nearly empty corridor. The remaining few girls that lingered in the halls at the end of the school day paid me no mind. Their gaze was for one person only—Will.

Why would you want them to look at you? You don't even like girls.

Most of the time, I was invisible to everyone. A nobody until the bullies decided to humiliate me.

Will, on the other hand, was someone everyone noticed—boys and girls. It wasn't just his size that drew their attention; it was his sheer magnetism. It was captivating in so many ways. Add in the fact he was a genuinely nice person, able to laugh at himself and he became irresistible.

Whatever Will was thinking was masked as he turned back to me. "I'll speak with your brother. I'm sure we can come up with a plan."

My stomach churned. "Plan for what?" I squeaked out, balling my hands into fists to stop myself from covering my mouth like a complete dork.

"Don't you worry that pretty little blond head," he muttered distractedly, his hand touching that same blond head as he ran his fingers through my curls.

He's your brother's best friend, nothing more. He's straight and would never be interested in you.

My shoulders slumped at the thought and I had to work hard to stop my lips from turning down at the corners.

"Let's go. I'll walk you home to make sure you don't get yourself into any more trouble. Your brothers would kick my ass if you did." His fingers tugged once more at my hair before releasing it and strolling away, with me having to run to keep up with the length of his strides.

See, he's only helping you because of your brothers, not for any other reason.

A boy could dream; there was no harm in that.

BOOKS BY THE AUTHOR

Standalone

When Fake Changed Everything
Christmas beyond Christmas
The Elves and the Bondage Daddy (Grim and Sinister Delights Book 5)

Series

The Potters Creek Series

A Christmas Wish (book one)

The App Series

The App: Daddy kink (book one)
The App: Littles (book two)
The App: Puppy play (book three) - January 2021

The Flamingo Bar Series

Always More (book one)
The Little Side of Me (book two)
3 is the magic number (book three) - February 2021

La Trattoria Di Amore Series

Puzzle Pieces (book one)
Dominated but not Subdued (book two)

The Playroom Series

Mine, Body and Soul: Part One
Mine, Body and Soul: Part Two

Mine, Body and Soul: Part Three
Ferron's Journey: Damaged Part One (book four)
Ferron's Journey: Hidden Part Two (book five)
Ferron's Journey: Revelation Part Three (book six)
Mine, Body and Soul Trilogy
Ferron's Journey Trilogy

The Billionaire Playground Series

Property of a Billionaire (Book one)

The Manx Cat Guardians Series

Where it all Began: Origins (Book 1)
Seeing Beyond the Scars (Book 2)
Destiny Collides Past and Present (Book 3)
Searching for a Soul to Love (Book 4)
The 12 Disasters of Christmas (Book 5)
Laws of Attraction (Book 6)
The Teacher's Boy (Book 7)
Boxset

Audio Books

Mine, Body and Soul, Part One: The Playroom Series
Mine, Body and Soul, Part Two: The Playroom Series
Mine, Body and Soul, Part Three: The Playroom Series
Daddy Kink: The App (book one)
Always More: The Flamingo Bar (book one)
When Fake Changed Everything
Ferron's Journey: Damaged Part One
Ferron's Journey: Hidden Part Two

ABOUT THE AUTHOR

Hi all,

My name is Jayne and I live in the Isle of Man. A tiny place in the Irish sea. It's an island steeped in folklore and history and just begs to have stories written about it, and one of my first inspirations. Over the last few years that has changed and now I find inspiration everywhere.

I'm an eclectic kinda girl so I've written contemporary and historical gay romance with a paranormal twist, daddy kink, fake boyfriends, out for you and enemies to lovers. My head is so full of ideas. I never know where it will take me next. I had a twelve book plan for 2020 and I smashed it and will release fourteen books and already I've a few new ones bubbling inside me waiting to be written 😊

I hope you have enjoyed this book, and if you are in need of more, then you can find all my other books, on Amazon and in KU.

If you would like to give me any feedback or just have any questions, go ahead and friend me on Facebook, and I would be happy to answer anything. Well, almost anything. I hope you enjoyed this book as it was a little different for me. If you would also like to leave a review, then I would love to read your thoughts.

Thank you for taking the time to be part of my dream.

JP SAYLE

www.ingramcontent.com/pod-product-compliance
Lightning Source LLC
Chambersburg PA
CBHW020821180626
46814CB00001B/62

* 9 7 8 1 9 1 4 0 7 7 0 1 2 *